"Who is out there?" Sarah whispered.

"I can make out two men. Three maybe."

"The police?" Her heart leaped as she sawed away at the bands around his ankle. "Rodriguez must have figured out what happened and sent help."

Jett stared into the sunlight. "Uh-uh."

Sarah worked frantically with the blade, freeing his ankles. "Jett, what are you thinking? Who are those men?"

"EODs have a motto," he said slowly. "Always prepare for the worst."

"How could this situation get any worse?"

Jett put his bound hands on her shoulder and held on, as if he could somehow anchor her there away from the danger. She reached for his hands to try to release them from the zip tie. "Jett?" she asked frantically. "What is it?"

"I don't know, but I've got that feeling."

"What feeling?"

"The kind of feeling I get right before something blows up."

Dana Mentink is an award-winning author of Christian fiction. Her novel *Betrayal in the Badlands* won a 2010 RT Reviewers' Choice Best Book Award, and she was pleased to win the 2013 Carol Award for *Lost Legacy*. She has authored more than a dozen Love Inspired Suspense novels. Dana loves feedback from her readers. Contact her via her website at danamentink.com.

Books by Dana Mentink

Love Inspired Suspense

Pacific Coast Private Eyes

Dangerous Tidings
Seaside Secrets
Abducted

Rookie K-9 Unit

Seek and Find

Wings of Danger

Hazardous Homecoming
Secret Refuge

Stormswept

Shock Wave
Force of Nature
Flood Zone

Treasure Seekers

Lost Legacy
Dangerous Melody
Final Resort

Visit the Author Profile page at Harlequin.com for more titles.

ABDUCTED

DANA MENTINK

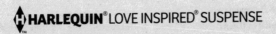

HARLEQUIN® LOVE INSPIRED® SUSPENSE

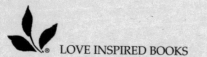

Recycling programs
for this product may
not exist in your area.

LOVE INSPIRED BOOKS

ISBN-13: 978-0-373-44778-7

Abducted

These things I have spoken unto you, that in me
ye might have peace. In the world ye shall have tribulation:
but be of good cheer; I have overcome the world.
–John 16:33

To Laurie, Shelley and Lindsay,
those darling three that have my back and fill my life
with the kind of love that only sisters can give.

ONE

Sarah Gallagher stood frozen in shock as Dominic Jett lurched through the clinic door, a limp body draped over his shoulder. The hot Mexican sun etched his bleeding face in golden fire. Why was he here in her clinic? She must be seeing things.

Peering at Sarah through swollen eyes, Jett sighed. "I really hate hospitals." His legs buckled and he dropped to his knees, letting his burden slide to the floor. His collapse finally jerked Sarah from her frozen shock.

She ran to the men, Juanita two steps behind her. Juanita called for their teenage helper to summon her father, the doctor, from the next village. Somehow she and Juanita wrestled the two men onto cots. It was a harder job with Jett, who was six feet five inches of ornery muscle and bone. He might not be in the navy anymore, but he kept his fighting trim. Sarah examined him, pleased to see his eyelids flicker open, revealing the chocolate-brown eyes that haunted her dreams, now hazed with pain. As they slowly opened, she recalled being lost in those eyes, her high school sweetheart, her everything. She blinked away the memory. "Can you tell me your name?" she asked.

"George Washington," he said, pushing her hands away. "I'm okay. Stop poking me."

Typical. He was the same stubborn, reckless man she'd known since they'd gone steady nine years before, except...different, as if the soul inside him had hardened into granite. She'd heard a rumor that he was working on a dive boat near the health clinic where she was completing her last medical mission, but she hadn't believed it. "Just hold still and let me check your pupils at least. What happened? Did you say the wrong thing to the wrong guy again?"

"For your information, I saved that scrawny dude over there from the three men trying to beat him senseless. I was trying to be a do-gooder, like you." His tone dripped with sarcasm. "See where that got me?"

She would not rise to take the bait, not now. Instead she pressed a wad of cotton to the cut on his forehead, her fingers grazing the strong bones of his cheek. He winced.

"Sorry," she said, her stomach tightening at the intensity in his eyes. "Hold this while I get some disinfectant," she commanded, pressing his fingers to the cotton, trying not to let the feel of his hand distract her. "Did you get hit on the head?" A blow on top of the injury she knew he'd sustained in his navy service could prove deadly.

His eyes narrowed, as if he knew exactly what she was thinking. "Just help him. I'm okay."

"Jett..."

He sat up, wincing again. "I said I'm okay. Go minister to someone else."

He was pushing her away like she'd done to him so many years ago. The lump in her throat surprised her. "Jett..."

An engine noise drew her to the door. She peeked out, heart dropping into her shoes at the sight of three men getting out of their truck. If she had any doubts about their intent, one look at what they carried told her the truth—one held a machete and the others baseball bats.

The tallest of them looked up, gave her a lazy smile. She slammed the door and dropped the bar across it. At least there were already stout beams in place covering most of the windows, an effort to keep away thieves.

Jett sat up. "What?"

"Three men," was all she could get past her terrified lips. Jett dived off the table and started to drag a heavy file cabinet in front of the door. She went to help him, pulse thundering.

"I got this," he snapped. "Go check the back."

Though she knew the back door was locked and secure, she raced to the rear of the small clinic, where there was a single window covered with shutters instead of barred to allow for ventilation. As she watched, the shutters were ripped aside and a man's arm plunged through the gap where the window had been raised a few inches. She skidded to a stop, shoes squeaking on the tile. While she looked desperately around to find something to use to fight him off, he cranked the window frame up and stuck his head inside. His eyes were red rimmed, wild, as if he was under the influence of drugs or alcohol or just plain hatred. There was an ugly purple bruise darkening his cheekbone—probably courtesy of Dominic Jett, she surmised.

She grabbed a teakettle from the stove and swung it as hard as she could. The man grunted, protecting his head with his crooked arm. His thin lips contorted in anger. He grabbed at her, catching her by the wrist and twisting until she dropped the kettle, gasping in pain. She could feel his hot breath on her face as he pulled her close, struggling to both get in the window and hold onto her.

If he managed to make it inside, they would all be

dead, she had no doubt. His grip was so hard she felt her fingers start to go numb. With his other hand, he reached inside to grab for her hair.

She struggled to pull away, jostling a pitcher of disinfecting fluid with two pairs of surgical scissors soaking inside. The pitcher was inches from her grasp, and she strained to reach it. Muscles pulled tight and her neck aching with the effort, she finally grasped the handle. She heaved it sideways at the man, dousing him with the contents. Eyes stinging, he pulled back just enough for her to slam the window and lock it.

She expected him to grab the nearest rock and use it to smash the glass to pieces. Her mouth fell open in surprise as she saw him run away. Panting, trying valiantly to make her lungs start to work properly again, she returned on wobbly legs to the front room.

Juanita turned frightened eyes on her. "They've left, for now."

"Why?" she managed, the terror making her tongue slow and unwieldy.

She soon saw for herself what had discouraged them as Jett let in a uniformed police officer. Don Rodriguez, Sarah knew, the commandant of the tiny Mexican village. She offered a relieved greeting, which he returned politely. Rodriguez stood, hands clasped behind his back, heavy brows twitching as he took in every detail of Jett and the unconscious stranger.

"There were men outside," Sarah said between gasps. "They attacked Jett and they were about to break in here when you arrived."

He shot a disdainful look at Jett. "It seems you have found trouble. Again."

Jett wiped the sweat off his forehead. "This time, it found me. I was returning from picking up a fuel filter a couple miles down the road and I came upon three guys beating on this one." He jutted his chin at the unconscious man. "They were trying to force him into their truck."

"Does he have any identification?" the officer asked.

Juanita handed him a wallet she'd taken out of the victim's pocket. "It says his name is Del Young."

Sarah thought the officer's mouth tightened at the name, but perhaps it was her imagination. Her nerves were still firing too erratically to trust her judgment. "Do you know him?"

"No. He is a stranger to me." He looked at Jett. "And the men beating him? They showed up here?"

Jett confirmed with a nod.

"What do you know of them?"

"Three guys, short, stocky, plenty strong. One was missing part of his pinky finger."

Now there was no mistaking the nervous look that stole over Rodriguez's face. "I will look into this matter. Best to let this man go."

"Go?" Sarah gaped. "He's unconscious. He needs to be flown to a hospital before those thugs return to kill him."

Rodriguez cocked his head, weighing his reply. "These men, the ones you fought," he said to Jett, "they work for Antonio Beretta."

Sarah felt her stomach flip over.

"Yeah? Who's that?" Jett said.

Sarah gaped. "How could you have lived here for a month and run a dive business and not know Antonio Beretta?"

Jett pulled the bloody cotton from his forehead and tossed it in the trash can. "I'm not the neighborhood busybody. I try to mind my own business." He gave her a sly smile. "But it's nice to know you've been keeping track of my life. I didn't know you'd paid attention to when I'd arrived."

She rolled her eyes. "Beretta's a very wealthy, very powerful man," she said. "We treated one of his victims just before you arrived."

"Victims?"

"Someone who crossed him." *And would never cross him again*, she thought with a shiver. "Beretta runs drugs."

"Rumors," Rodriguez said.

"More than rumors." Sarah looked at her patient. "You think we should leave this man because Beretta is after him for some reason?"

"This is a local concern. You should not be involved."

"I'm a medical missionary, and he's injured. I'm already involved."

Rodriguez stared at her. "You have done good things for the people in my town, so I telling you this out of gratitude. If you are in Beretta's way, he will kill you and everyone with you, and no one, not even God Himself, will be able to save you."

Her chin went up. "God brought me here for a reason, and I'm not going to leave my patient to die," she snapped.

Rodriguez shrugged. "If Beretta is involved, he is already a dead man. Take him back where you found him and leave him there."

Sarah stared him right in the face. "I'm not going to do that."

"As you wish. It is no matter to me."

"Well, aren't you going to investigate?" Her cheeks flushed hot. "We need some protection, at least."

"I have other matters to attend to."

"You're not even going to do your job?" she demanded.

He pointed a finger at her. "Please do not tell me about my job. You have no right to direct affairs here."

"I am a part of this community."

He arched an eyebrow. "Isn't it true that you are due to leave next week, Senorita Gallagher?"

She didn't answer.

"It is fact, is it not? Your mission in Playa del Oro—" his tone dripped with derision "—is nearly complete, and then you will fly away to your comfortable life in America and our lives here will continue on."

"That doesn't mean—" she started.

"You are an outsider, in case you have forgotten," Rodriguez said, "and now you are on your own." He whirled on his heel and exited the clinic.

Sarah walked to the door and watched him drive away. "He's not going to do a thing," she said. "Unbelievable."

"But understandable," Jett said, "if Beretta is such a bad dude."

She stared outside, wondering when the men would return. "No, it isn't, not to me."

"Ah, Sarah, always the idealist," Jett said, and she thought there was a tinge of longing in the words under the sarcasm. It confused her, and she turned back toward her patient.

The man on the other cot lay completely still. He was probably in his mid-thirties, thin, with blond hair that hung in sweat-soaked clumps almost down to his chin. Her heart went out to him. A stranger to Playa del Oro finds himself the victim of a violent attack. Not so unusual anymore in a town that struggled with a flourishing drug trade, poverty, gang violence and corruption. She'd grown to love the town and the people here in her last two medical missions. But Rodriguez was right, she was scheduled to leave, and this time she would not return, since she was starting down a new path, retiring from nursing to join the family private investigation business.

Young's cheeks were swollen and bruised. She wondered who he was, if his family was worrying about him, if he had a wife somewhere standing by, waiting for the phone to ring. Was he a father? Her heart squeezed. She knew how huge a hole a father's death could leave in a family.

Juanita's face was grave. "He's got a serious head injury. There's a laceration on his arm and cheek that need stitches."

And they had no CAT scan machine, not here in the Playa del Oro mission clinic. "We're going to need to move him to Puerto Rosado as soon as we can stabilize him. The hospital there can handle this."

Jett was sitting up now. "I can take him up the coast in my boat. We have to get him and you out of here before the Three Stooges return."

She bit her lip. "We'll find someone to fly us. It will be faster."

"No, it won't. The airport is an hour away, and you're going to have to pay a king's ransom for a pilot, not to mention they'll soak you for fuel."

He was right, of course, but she wasn't ready to admit that to him. "For now we'll monitor his vitals, stitch him up and wait for the doctor to check him out. We'll keep the doors and windows locked."

"That is a ridiculous plan," he snapped.

"I didn't ask for your opinion."

"I'm offering it, free of charge. You can't stay here and…" Jett's head jerked up. He made for the front door again and looked out. "Too late," he said. "They're back, and this time they're not going to leave until they finish the job."

There was a sound of shattering terra cotta, a baseball bat decimating the pots of bougainvillea on the porch. Then they began to batter down the door.

The bat struck so hard the walls shook.

In spite of the urgency, Jett admired the fire in Sarah's hazel eyes, the firm tilt of her delicate chin as she'd tried to figure out how to save her patient. He attempted to shake off the ringing in his ears that had roared to life again when he'd taken on the thugs. Great. He'd finally overcome the seizures, leftovers from the grievous injury that had ruined his navy career and reduced him to being the dive master on a rinky-dink boat in Tijuana. Now the ringing was back.

He ground his teeth together. *You'll overcome this, too.*

The next crack of the bat against the door sounded like cannon fire. Both women jumped.

Jett tried for what he figured was a reasonable tone. "We've got to get him out of here."

"It's not safe to move him. He might be bleeding internally," Sarah said.

"He's going to be bleeding externally, too, if we don't move, and so will the rest of us." Another pot shattered outside.

She trembled, the crown of her blond head barely brushing his chin as they hauled the kitchen table over to join the file cabinet. "Just because Marco sicced you on me doesn't mean I have to take orders from you," she fired off.

He tensed. "Marco didn't sic me on you. He asked me to make sure you were okay during your missionary stint, and since I was in Tijuana, it was easy for me to make my way to this part of the coast for a while." A partial truth. Even if his bank account hadn't been down to his last hundred bucks, he still wouldn't have taken the job so close to Sarah if Marco Quidel, his mentor and a protector to the Gallagher sisters, hadn't asked him to. He wouldn't let Marco down for anything. *You're a sap, Jett, for all your tough-guy moves.*

One of the men was shouting now, whacking his baseball bat against the walls of the clinic as he looked for windows or unlocked doors.

Sarah went pale. "Will anyone come to help us?"

Jett braced himself against the next blow as boots began to smash against the flimsy door.

"Sorry, Sarah Gal. We're on our own."

TWO

Jett saw Sarah flinch, her slight frame tensing as if an electric current had passed through it. "The same men?" she whispered.

"Beretta's guys, all right." His gaze slid to the unconscious man on the table. Like the cop said, they'd come back to finish the job.

One of the tiny windows set high up in the walls shattered, and a rock clunked onto the floor along with a shower of glass. "Get back," he yelled. Fortunately, the tiny opening was too small for the thugs to get through, but their message was clear.

Coming for you.

It was just a matter of moments now.

Sarah raced to the back, only to return seconds later. "There's a guy out there again, too. He's almost gotten through. I wedged a chair under the handle, but it won't hold for long."

"Any other exits?"

Sarah looked at Juanita who nodded. "There's an underground exit off the cellar, but we've never had to use it before."

"No time like the present," Jett said.

"What if it's boarded up?"

"Then we kick it open. Take Young down there and get out. I'll hold them off as long as I can." Their blows were already causing the heavy wood to shudder.

"I can't just leave you here," Sarah said, mouth twisted.

"I'll be right behind you. Get moving."

"But…"

One booted foot punched through the wood and slammed against the metal file drawers, the impact vibrating his spine. It was probably the time for calm reasoning and diplomacy, but he had none to offer. Besides, in his experience the best way to combat fear was a commanding officer barking orders at you. "Now, Sarah," he thundered. "Go now."

Sarah and Juanita threw a bag of supplies together and loaded Young onto a stretcher, strapping him onto the canvas frame. Juanita heaved open the trapdoor in the floor and crawled down first, guiding the stretcher into a near vertical position with Sarah on the other end.

"Jett…" Sarah said, green-gold eyes wide with fear. He could see now that her hands were shaking. Badly.

"Go on," he said, trying for a gentler tone that was still persuasive. He wasn't sure how hard he should push her, how strong she was after being in the hospital so long after the accident that killed her father, but there wasn't much choice at the moment. She'd always been a strong person, and he had to hope that was still the case. "I'll be right behind you."

He could see her jaw muscles tighten. She flashed him a determined, almost defiant look—which he loved—before she climbed into the hole with her end of the stretcher. It couldn't have been easy, but she managed the thing. *Sarah Gallagher, you still got your spunk.*

He shoved his back against the file cabinet to make the inevitable breach take as long as possible. The metal slammed against his shoulder blades, nearly taking him off his feet. As much as he longed for a rematch, he was not going to win another fight against these three, not now, when he was still bruised and sore from their last encounter. The thought rankled him. He was going to lose. Again. He detested losing, always had.

Fine, he thought. If he was going down, at least he'd buy time for the women to get out with their patient. He looked around for something, anything useful. No weapons, no tools. What he wouldn't give for a baseball bat or a shovel.

The jug of hand sanitizer. He smiled. Alcohol based, classified as class I flammable liquid substance with a flash point of less than one hundred degrees. Not as satisfying as disposing of small arms ammo with copious amounts of gasoline and thermite, but it might gain them a few minutes. Of course, Sarah would never condone the damage it would cause, but lives were more important than property and beggars couldn't be choosers.

He seized the jug and a handful of towels. Throwing the towels down on the center of the floor, he dumped on the gel, two gallons of it. Then he grabbed a box of matches and lit it. It took a few seconds for the alcohol in the gel to catch. When it flamed to life, he dumped on a pile of paper towels, just for some extra oomph, and soon the smoke filled the small building, tickling his nose and stinging his eyes. Excellent.

He heard the creak of metal as their boots finally crashed through the door and started to work on shoving the file cabinet aside. In the back the sound of splintering wood indicated Sarah's barricade was near failing. One more minute and Beretta's men would walk right into the wall of smoke. His nerves were dancing with adrenaline. Fire, smoke, danger, risk. Good times.

Enjoy the campfire, gentlemen. With one last smile, he raced to the trapdoor and let himself down into the darkness, closing it firmly behind him.

Sarah felt like her lungs would explode in her chest as she and Juanita bumped through the damp earthen basement with their stricken patient. They tried their best to sync their steps to avoid jostling him too much.

Please, God, don't let the exit be blocked.

She strained to hear the sound of running feet above her. Fear coiled like a live snake in her stomach. Jett was battered, alone with three men, and he had the same superhero attitude he'd had all his life. It was the same attitude that caused him to take a dare one stormy evening to jump a riverbed on his motorcycle. That hadn't ended well. She still remembered her fear at seeing him there in the hospital bed, still and unresponsive. What had she been thinking leaving him in the clinic by himself? But how could she abandon her patient?

"Juanita, I can't hold the stretcher much longer," she panted.

"Here's the door." Sweating and gasping, they eased past stacks of boxes. Juanita heaved a heavy wooden bar aside and swung the door open. Brilliant June sunlight nearly blinded them, wrapping them in the sizzling heat of a Mexican afternoon.

They stepped out to find themselves in the weed-filled space that doubled as a parking lot for those few who were fortunate enough to have a vehicle. Incredibly, the doctor's old, battered truck was there. He'd opted to walk to the nearby village to save the cost of the fuel. Sarah almost cried with relief.

"Quick," she said. "We'll load him in. Then I'm going back to help Jett."

"No," Juanita said, frightened eyes opened wide.

Sarah did not listen. Instead she helped Juanita ease Young into the bed of the truck. Juanita got behind the wheel and fingered the visor where her father always left the keys.

"Start it up," Sarah commanded. "Drive a mile down the road and wait. If we don't come in ten minutes, take him to your father."

Juanita's lips pinched with fear. "Beretta's men will kill you both."

Sarah steeled her spine against the wild fear. "I'm not going to leave Jett. He's our patient, too."

Juanita clung to her hand until Sarah pulled away. Juanita started the engine, and Sarah prayed the attackers would not hear the noise.

She raced back to basement, noting the smell of smoke in the air.

She wanted to yell for Jett, but she was afraid of attracting any attention, so she crept on, stopping every few feet to listen. The tang of smoke was stronger now, which hastened her pace toward the ladder. They wouldn't dare burn down the clinic, would they? In the back of her mind, she still could not believe someone was intent on murdering Del Young.

So naive, Sarah. Your father was murdered. Why not Del? Why not you? It had been a mere six months since the car she was driving was forced off the road and her detective father was killed. It had required a full four weeks in the hospital for her body to recover from the injuries she'd sustained in the accident. Justice had been served, thanks to Marco and her sisters and it had given her a desire to earn her detective license while she lay in the hospital recovering. But she'd insisted on fulfilling her promise to do her final missionary service in Playa del Oro. Would she pay for that decision with her life? Forcing herself to move beyond the paralyzing terror, she'd just put her hand on the first rung when a calloused palm sealed off her mouth. She thrashed her arms and tried to clamp her teeth on her assailant.

"Stop biting and don't scream," Jett breathed, holding her tightly. "Or they'll be down here in two seconds."

Relief made her knees go weak.

He eased his hand away, and she could not help wrapping him in a tight hug. His hands went reflexively around her waist, and he chuckled softly. "You won't think I deserve a hug when you find out about my little diversion," he whispered, lips grazing her ear. "Not that I'm complaining, mind you."

Her good sense returned, and she shoved him away. "I was just…relieved that you weren't dead."

"You and me both," he said, taking her hand and urging her back toward the exit. "That would have ruined my whole day. Keep moving. We don't have much of a head start. Where's your helper?"

Sarah told her the plan she'd concocted.

"That was savvy," he said.

"You sound surprised."

"Didn't think you had the street smarts to come up with a plan like that."

"Just because I'm not a tough guy like you doesn't mean I can't think on my feet."

"Yeah, you were thinking just fine when you dumped me in high school."

Heat seared her cheeks as she yanked her hand away. "Maybe this isn't the greatest time to go into our past relationship failures."

"Your failure, not mine. I wasn't the one who walked away. You broke up with me, remember?"

She ground her teeth together to keep from firing off an angry retort. The light traced the exit door just ahead of them. They burst through the sultry air into the sunlight. Darting a look back, she saw drifts of smoke coming from the clinic. In the distance came the shouts of the men inside and a clamor of Spanish as the townspeople came running with buckets to put out the fire.

He grabbed her hand again and tugged her into action.

Keeping their heads down, they ran along the road, kicking up pockets of dust, heading for the cluster of palm trees where Juanita must be waiting.

"Just how big a diversion did you create?" Sarah panted, turning to look back again at the smoking clinic.

"It's still standing, isn't it?" Jett said. "There she is." They ran to the idling truck and leaped in the back next to the patient. Juanita sat ramrod straight behind the wheel, worrying her lower lip between her teeth.

"Drive to the dock," Jett commanded.

"They'll find you there," Juanita said. "Come with me until it's dark. I have a place we can hide that Beretta's men don't know about. My father will treat Mr. Young there. You can sneak out after sunset."

"But the police…" Sarah said.

Juanita put the truck in gear. "They are of no help."

"She's right," Jett said. "The cops aren't going to keep this guy safe from Beretta—Rodriguez told you as much. We have to get out of here, head for US waters. The coast guard will intercept us, and we can tell them the whole story."

Sarah shook her head. "We can't just run away. We have to tell the doctor, arrange to have another nurse assigned, talk to the chief of police…"

"I will do all that," Juanita said quietly.

"No," Sarah said. "Not alone. You won't be safe."

"This village is my home," Juanita said. "I'm not leaving. My father and I will keep the clinic open and talk to the police, even though it will do no good."

"I can't…"

"Yes," she said, catching Sarah's eye in the rearview mirror. "You must."

Sarah had worked with Juanita for the three months she'd been at the clinic, and the woman had always been quiet, even tempered. The iron in her voice was new, or perhaps Sarah had not taken the time to recognize it before.

"Okay," she finally said. "We'll escape after dark." As they sped out of town toward Juanita's house, Sarah prayed darkness would come quickly.

THREE

It was nearly four when they arrived with their ailing patient at a small brick building with a crooked front door and a corrugated metal roof. Jett figured it had been a little café at one time, but now the windows were shuttered and the front step sagged. Like the town itself, it seemed to be sinking under the crushing weight of the poverty all around it.

He climbed from the truck and tried to stretch out some of the stiffness in his back, but the pain from his bruised body put an end to that. *You're not an eighteen-year-old kid anymore*, he thought. *There's a price to be paid now for putting your body on the line.* Didn't matter. He'd pay it anyway, regardless of the consequences. He'd never hesitated to take the savage blows intended for his mother.

Why don't you hit me? he'd taunted his father countless times when dear old Dad had come home stinking of whiskey. *Leave her alone*, he'd shouted, like a lion tamer luring a beast with an offering of fresh meat. He shook the thought away, wondering if he'd ever be able to rid himself of those memories.

A one-eared dog trotted up, sniffing the group as they unloaded Young from the truck, offering a tentative yip.

Another hungry soul, scrounging anywhere for anything. Jett stooped to give the bony head a pat. "Sorry I don't have any food for you, boy."

The dog wagged its tail anyway as Juanita hurried to open the door. "Inside, quickly," she said.

The interior was molten, warmer even than the air outside. Immediately they were bathed in sweat. Jett and Sarah carried Young inside and laid his stretcher on a long wooden table. Sarah loosened his straps, and he moaned. His eyes flickered open, but he was clearly out of it, forehead lined with pain and eyes sunken, skin waxy.

"He needs IV fluids," Sarah said, rummaging in her bag.

Juanita nodded. "While you administer them, I will go get us some food and water."

"Want me to go with you?" Jett said. "What if Beretta's men followed us?"

Juanita flashed a quick smile. "Then I will be quick, and on the lookout like Detective Sarah."

Sarah laughed, a sound that was at odds with their dire circumstances, like the peal of cheerful music in a dungeon. "I left my magnifying glass back in Coronado. Right now, I'm Nurse Sarah."

"Probably a more helpful occupation for the circumstances." Juanita frowned at the patient and sped out the door, closing it behind her.

Jett watched Sarah fuss over Young. "So how exactly are you going to be both a nurse and a detective?"

Her attention was fixed on her work. "I've decided to give up nursing after this mission and help full-time with the detective agency."

That surprised him. She'd always been passionate about her occupation. "Yeah? Why did you decide on that?"

"Because I guess I've had enough of death," she said.

The expression, that sadness in her voice, made him want to fold her in his arms. The experience of losing her father had changed her, taking some of the brilliance away from her smile. But, hey, he thought uncharitably, she had her God. Wasn't He supposed to protect people like her? Still, it grieved him that she should be touched by tragedy of that magnitude. Some people deserved the bitter stuff that life dished out to them. Sarah did not.

As he puzzled over what to say, he made himself useful by holding the plastic tubing and handing Sarah the materials as she gloved up, applied the tourniquet, disinfected Young's arm with a small wipe and started the IV. He held up the bag of fluids as she released the tourniquet. A nail protruding from the wall served as a good place to hang it. Jett envied the liquid being pumped into Young. His own mouth was so dry he could hardly manage a swallow.

As she snapped off her gloves, she talked soothingly to Young, stroking his hand and wiping his brow with a clean cloth. Her patter was meant to be comforting, he supposed, but for Jett, it brought back too many memories, too many consoling platitudes that were intended to encourage him after the vehicle accident that left him with a serious head injury.

"Can I pray for you?" Sarah asked her patient.

Pray? The word made Jett bristle inside. She was living in a fantasy world, praying to a God who didn't listen or just didn't care, a fact he'd thought she would have learned after her accident. Either way, it sickened him. *Let's pray for your recovery*, the hospital chaplain had said to Jett a year ago. *Ask God to take away your pain.* He'd done neither, and what was more, He'd taken away Jett's career, the only light in Jett's life.

God wasn't some fairy-tale father who granted wishes. He created humans and left them to drown in their own misery, which wasn't any better than Jett's worthless earthly parent, currently serving time in prison. How could a smart girl like Sarah not see that for herself? He felt her gaze on him, and he looked away.

As Young's eyelids fluttered open again, he moaned, whispering something.

She bent closer to hear, her dark blond hair brushing the table. Young grasped her wrist, his mouth moving sporadically before he got the words out. "You're a detective?" he croaked.

"I've got a detective license," she said. "But don't worry. Right now, I'm your nurse. You're going to get some fluids, which will help you feel more comfortable, and we'll get you to a proper hospital."

"You've got to go find her," he murmured.

She shot Jett a look, and he moved closer. "What did you say, Mr. Young?"

He squeezed her wrist as a spasm of pain crossed his face and he struggled to sit up against Sarah's restraining hands.

"Find who?" Jett said.

Young's eyes suddenly rolled back in his head, and he collapsed back on the table.

Sarah checked his pulse and breathing. "He's hanging on by a thread. If we don't get him to a doctor soon, he's not going to make it." She pushed the sweat-soaked hair from his face and fanned him with a notepad from her bag. "What do you think he means by 'go find her'?"

Jett shrugged. "You're the detective. Your family's making quite a name for themselves in the investigation business."

"Marco's been filling you in?"

"He told me your sister recently cracked a case in Cobalt Cove."

She smiled. "How sweet that you stay up-to-date on Gallagher family business."

"I don't," he said, more severely than he'd meant to. "But seeing as how you and your sisters run an investigation firm, do your thing. Solve this guy's mystery."

"How am I supposed to do that under the present circumstances?"

"Don't look at me—I'm just a diver. But it sounds like you just got yourself a case, Detective."

Jett was clearly mocking her, so she ignored the remark. "Mr. Young? Can you hear me?" But he was unconscious. Go find whom? Was whoever he was looking for the reason he'd been beaten? The cause of Beretta's relentless attention?

There was no sense in talking it over with Jett. He'd gone to the back window to wrench loose one of the boards, allowing a breeze to waft in. Delicious, she thought, lifting the hair off her neck and tying it into a ponytail with a piece of gauze. If she'd had a moment more to pack, she'd have been much better prepared, but as it was, she'd only tossed in basic medical supplies, her passport and one granola bar. At the bottom of the bag were two precious bottles of water. Thirst clawed at her. As much as she wanted to rip off the cap and guzzle some of the water, she was uncertain about their upcoming journey and she thought it best to save it. Maybe she should offer a bottle to Jett.

He'd stepped out into the back, which was nothing more than a scruff of weed-covered ground, dry and parched. He knelt to play with the one-eared dog who was so skinny she could see his ribs. Jett stroked his big hands tenderly over the dog's delicate frame. Those same hands had caressed her face with a featherlight touch.

She was transported back in time to their first date, a trip to the ice cream parlor and a walk on the beach. He'd found a shell for her in the sand, a delicate white scallop tinged with the fiery glow of a sunrise on the inside. Shyly, he'd offered it to her.

It's perfect, he'd said. *Like you.*

She remembered his arms embracing her, a bittersweet reminder. So much anger and so much heart wrapped up in one maddening man, she thought.

"Here," she said, handing him a bottle of water.

"Thanks." He twisted the cap and poured a small amount into his hand. The dog lapped it up eagerly. Jett lifted the bottle to his lips, eyeing her before he put it to his mouth. "Hang on. Did you get some?"

"I'm okay."

He shook his head and handed it back to her. "You drink half."

"I don't need any."

"Fine. Then I don't, either."

She folded her arms. "You're a patient. Patients before nurses."

"You're a woman," he snapped. "Women before men."

He folded his arms to match hers, and she knew he wasn't going to give in. "You're infuriating, you know that?" she said, snatching the bottle.

"Funny how many people tell me that."

She gulped, restraining herself from downing it all. Even though it was warm, the water tasted delectable. Then she handed it to him, and he drained the rest. They stood in the yard, trying to find some relief from the stifling heat, until Juanita called from inside. She'd returned with a bag of savory-smelling food and a clay jug. Sarah's mouth watered.

"My cousin makes excellent *chilaquiles*. There is no meat today, but it is still good, I think."

"It smells divine," Sarah said.

She handed them plastic forks, metal plates covered with foil and two paper cups, which she filled with water. Jett raised his to his mouth, drinking it in two swallows.

Sarah set the plate aside and folded her hands to pray. Juanita did the same. Jett, she noticed, stepped away, arms crossed over his broad chest, until they were done.

Under the foil were quarters of fried corn tortilla covered with a green salsa and topped with slices of raw onion. A humble dish, generously shared by people who had little to give. There could be no greater blessing than that, Sarah thought.

There was a period of quiet while they devoured the luscious meal and drained the jug to the dregs. Jett offered one of his tortillas to the dog, who happily gobbled it up.

"Did you get word to your father?" Sarah said.

Juanita frowned. "Yes. He will meet us here."

"How will he avoid Beretta's men?" Jett said. "They're probably swarming the town right about now."

"He will be all right," she said, turning away to gather up the remnants of the meal. Sarah helped her wipe out the dishes as best they could and pack them up to be returned to Juanita's cousin.

"You have been very kind, Juanita," Sarah said. "I know this is above and beyond. You've been so brave."

Juanita turned to face her. "No," she said, voice cracking. "I haven't. Oh, please forgive me, Sarah."

The stricken look on her face started alarm bells ringing in Sarah's brain. "Forgive you for what?"

Her lips trembled. "I…"

Jett drew close. "What did you do?"

The door swung open. On the threshold stood the men from the clinic, dark haired, sweating through their T-shirts, two holding bats.

The taller one smiled and turned to his partner as he looked at Young.

"Good thing for you he's still alive. I told you not to hit him on the head—you might have killed him." Then he jutted his chin in Juanita's direction. "Go. Your father is safe. He will be released now that you have done your part."

Sarah looked at Juanita in horror.

"You sold us out?" Jett said.

"I'm sorry." Tears sprang up in her eyes, and she wrung her hands. "My father called my cell phone while I was waiting in the truck. They will kill him if I do not do as they ask. I could not sacrifice his life for yours."

Jett shook his head in disgust, but Sarah gripped Juanita's hand. "You didn't have a choice."

"Forgive me," Juanita murmured.

Sarah nodded. "You did what you had to do. It's okay."

"Go," said one of the men to Juanita. "And speak to no one of this." She hurried out, a hand pressed to her mouth, stifling her sobs.

The taller man bobbed a chin at Young. "It is fortunate for us that we did not kill him before. Senor Beretta would be most unhappy. Thank you, Senorita Gallagher, for keeping him alive."

She stuck up her chin and glared at him. "He needs a hospital."

"He will get plenty of medical attention until his usefulness is over. As for you two…" He shook his head. "You were clever to escape the clinic."

Jett smiled. "And you were stupid to fall for it."

The taller man lashed out so quickly Sarah almost didn't see it. His bat connected with Jett's stomach, sending him sprawling backward.

She screamed and dropped to her knees next to him.

"Home-run hit, Miguel," the leader said.

Jett sucked in a breath and groaned. She pressed her hands to his broad chest. "Please don't antagonize him," she whispered. "Please."

Jett quirked a grin. "I'm just getting warmed up."

She helped him to his feet, determined to take action before Jett could say another word.

"Listen to me." She kept her voice calm, businesslike. "If Mr. Young is important to Senor Beretta, then he would want you to help get him to the hospital. We can get to the airport, fly him to Puerto Rosado. He needs a brain scan."

The man considered. "That is not for us to decide. We're taking him, and we no longer need your assistance."

Jett stepped forward, one hand clutched to his stomach. "Let her go," he grunted. "She's well-loved here in the village. You don't want to mess with her or there may be trouble. Release her, and she won't tell anyone about you."

Sarah could only gape. Since when was Jett her spokesman?

"I don't think so," the tall man said.

"You're making a mistake," Jett snapped.

This made both men laugh heartily. "Our only mistake was not bashing your brains in earlier."

Jett didn't flinch, but Sarah's whole body prickled in fear.

FOUR

The terrible command hung in the heated air.

Sarah's face went pale as sea foam, and she clenched her hands into fists.

Jett stared down the men. If they expected him to be intimidated, they would be disappointed. He shook his head with an exaggerated sigh. "I see intelligence doesn't rank high on the list of Senor Beretta's job requirements."

Miguel started forward again with the bat. "We should kill him now, Alex. Enough talk. Beat him until he begs for mercy."

Jett felt Sarah's hand clutching the back of his shirt.

It doesn't matter what they do to me, he wanted to tell her. *No one is ever going to see me beg.* He'd seen enough of that in his mother, and it left a vile taste in his mouth. Her pleading for his father to stop, to quit drinking, to stop the beatings, to leave off the behavior that turned their home into a war zone. None of her begging had made the slightest difference.

He refocused, ignoring the burning in his stomach from the bat blow. Sarah was the important one right now. Marco had charged him with her safety, so it was time to bluff. Big-time. "Young is on death's door, in case you haven't noticed. If you serve up a fresh corpse to your boss, he's not going to take that well, is he?"

"The coward's just talking to try to save himself." Miguel spat on the floor.

"A little testy, Miguel? Upset that I gave you that black eye earlier today? You shouldn't drop your left hand. I was trained by a navy boxing champion, so I'm afraid I had a big advantage." Marco had earned that championship honestly. The guy was a genius in the ring. He'd taught Jett plenty about fighting and life. Besides, it was a pleasure to rub salt in Miguel's wounded pride, even though he could feel the dread rolling off Sarah at his goading.

Miguel glowered. "I will crush your skull."

"Try," Jett said. "It will be a moment you'll never forget." Big talk, since Jett's head was pounding from the earlier fight and the bat strike had left him unable to draw a full breath. Still, there was enough anger burning through him that would fuel his muscles into delivering what his mouth had promised.

Miguel's face pinched with rage. "You will die slowly, American."

"And you will eat those words," Jett said, enunciating each and every syllable so there was no mistake. They were six inches from each other now. He could read the hatred simmering in Miguel's eyes. He hoped Miguel could see the same in his.

Alex held up a hand. "*Un momento.* Let me hear what this arrogant American says before we finish this."

Sarah sucked in a breath, and Miguel grudgingly eased back a pace.

"Young is going to die without Sarah's help—it's that simple," Jett said.

Alex shrugged. "We will get him medical assistance."

"Yeah? Where?"

"We do have hospitals here in our country, in case you were not aware." Alex's tone dripped with sarcasm.

"I am aware, and the closest one with an MRI machine is Puerto Rosado. There will be a lot of people there asking questions, forms to fill out, the victim being an American and all." Jett was guessing about Young's citizenship, but he saw in Alex's face that he'd hit the mark.

"The village doctor," the third man said. "We will make him do the treatments."

"He can't help," Sarah chimed in. "Young needs a brain scan. We don't have the equipment here to do that."

Jett saw Alex thinking it over. He made a show of looking at Young, who groaned softly. "Sounds pretty bad. He might even die before you get him to your truck, unless Sarah keeps up with the IVs and monitors his heart."

"I can't do it myself," she said quickly. "I need an assistant, since you sent Juanita away."

Alex waved at Miguel and his other companion. "We are not lacking for manpower."

"Jett's had navy medical training," Sarah cut in. "He knows what to do if Mr. Young has a seizure or goes into cardiac arrest, and he can administer an IV if necessary."

That much was true, but was it enough to convince Alex? The seconds ticked by in agonizing slow motion. Jett clenched his teeth. They had to let Sarah go with Young. It was the only way to keep her alive, at least until another escape avenue could present itself. He burned to go with her—she was too naive, too delicate to survive with these criminals—but if it was a choice between the two of them, he wanted her to live. The ferocity of his emotions surprised him, but then, he'd always longed for justice that never seemed to materialize. And Sarah—oh, how he'd longed for her.

It was not right for Sarah Gallagher to die here. She

was good, and she deserved a happy life. She'd certainly deserved better than a rebel like him. She'd been smart to cut him loose during their senior year in high school, though he'd never admit it. Nor would he confess how the pain of that breakup hurt worse than any physical wound he'd ever experienced.

I love you, Jett, but you're destroying yourself, and I just can't bear to watch.

He shut down the feelings. Just a mission. He owed Marco, and Marco loved Sarah like a sister. Get the job done and get her home safely. That was all.

Young began to cough violently at that moment, and Sarah hastened over. "Jett, help me roll him."

She could have performed the action fine by herself, but in order to make it look convincing, he eased Young onto his side, and the coughing turned to heavy gasps. Sarah looked helplessly at Alex. "His health is failing. Can't you see that?"

Alex considered. "It's a three-hour ride by truck from here to our destination."

Which is...? Jett wondered. Where did this Beretta station himself? Not in a poor village like Playa del Oro, certainly. Somewhere isolated enough to give the criminal his privacy and accommodations worthy of his drug lord status. "Has Beretta got a little compound in the mountains?" Jett guessed. No reaction from the goons. "Going to be rough terrain, huh? Did you guys get hold of an ambulance so we can get Young there without worsening his head injury? Or were you planning to throw a gravely injured man in the back of a truck and hope he survives?"

Again, no reaction except for a slight shifting from the third guy.

"Uh-huh, that's what I thought."

Alex came to a decision. "We will keep the nurse alive until we reach Senor Beretta."

"And the man?" Miguel said. "Surely we can help the nurse if she needs it. It is too dangerous to let him live."

Jett stared them down full-on. If they were expecting fear as they pronounced his sentence, they wouldn't get it.

There was a long pause. Sarah blanched, hazel eyes like gemstones, startling against her pale skin. Jett continued to assess. If they decided to kill him, he would take down as many as he could until he fell. It might give Sarah a chance to run, hide somewhere.

Alex considered, eyes shifting from Sarah to Jett. "Act in haste, repent in leisure. Isn't that the saying? Bind his hands and feet after they load Young into the truck. We'll take all three with us."

"But…" Miguel said.

Alex smiled. "I did not say you had to treat him gently, Miguel. Take some comfort in that, just don't disable him completely. Now!" Alex snapped. "You two carry Young to the truck, quickly. We do not wish to attract any more attention than we already have."

Jett let out a cautious breath. They'd scored a victory, even though it was only delaying the inevitable end. In his job as a navy explosive ordnance disposal technician, he'd learned how precious moments could be—seconds could mean the difference between a safe detonation and a catastrophe, going home to the woman who loved you or your life ending in a fine pink mist, according to the dark humor of the EODs.

They'd bought some moments. It would do for now.

He endured the blow Miguel gave him between the shoulder blades and helped Sarah gather up her supplies. Young moaned once more.

"It's okay, Mr. Young. We're going to take you somewhere now," Sarah said, her voice as cheerful as he figured she could make it. There was no response.

Jett wondered if they were taking Young out of the frying pan and dropping him straight into the flames. It was a mercy that the guy was too out of it to realize what was happening.

As Jett readied himself to lift the stricken man onto the stretcher, he was thunderstruck as Young gave Sarah a slow wink before he closed his eyes again.

Sarah struggled hard to keep her fear in check as they carried Young to the back of a delivery truck and climbed up after him. She knew she was going to be delivered into the hands of a murderous man who ruled by intimidation. It was dark inside, hot as a furnace, but a small amount of light shone through a slatted ventilation panel in the roof. She did not take her gaze off Young for a moment, but he made no further signs of consciousness. Had she imagined the wink? But the quickly concealed surprise on Jett's face indicated he'd witnessed the same thing. What if Young was not the helpless victim he appeared to be? Yet he was certainly not faking his injuries. The man was in dire medical straits, no question, but his last "fit" had been well timed and kept them both alive, at least for the next uncertain stretch of time.

Miguel sat on a wooden box lashed to the floor, a silent warden as the truck lurched away from the house where Juanita had made a deadly bargain for her father's life. Though Sarah knew Jett wouldn't see it the same way, the girl had not had a choice. What bargain would she have struck to save the lives of her family members? It was the kind of question that remained best unanswered.

Sarah tried to steady the stretcher against the heaving of the truck. On his knees, Jett attempted to help, though they'd tied his hands together in front of him with a plastic cord and done the same to his ankles. Helpless—all three of their fates were controlled by violent men with evil intentions.

She felt the tide of anger and darkness rise up inside her, fresh as it had been the moment when their car had been rammed by another six months prior, ending the life of her hero, her father. It was as if she could still feel the shards of glass flying around her, see her father's arm braced on the dash, his other holding protectively to her shoulder as they'd skidded out of control. The terrible shriek of metal still rang in her ears when she let it. Pain, darkness, medicines and surgeries, and then she'd woken to find the horror was not a dream. Her father was dead.

It was unjust, unfair, unacceptable. Her hands balled into tight fists. Wasn't her father's death enough for her to endure? And her sister Angela's recent encounter with a killer? How much was Sarah Gallagher expected to take? *How much, God?*

When it became too much, she forced a breath in and out, recalling the painful lesson she'd been learning since her father's death. How many hours had she lain in the hospital with a broken pelvis and a punctured lung wrestling with God? *It's not about what you do or don't deserve, Sarah Gallagher, it's about seeking Him.* Hard-won wisdom, excruciating to learn, difficult to hang onto. If it weren't for the rock-solid love and faith of her three sisters and her mother, she might never have made it.

She wondered if her sisters even knew she and Jett had been snatched. They might not, if Juanita had been coerced into silence. And the police would not report her gone if it meant crossing Beretta. There might be no one looking for them at all.

She kept her eyes closed speaking silently to God, who

she knew was there, even in the present terrifying circumstances. When she opened her eyes again, Jett was watching her, one eyebrow quirked.

"Still thinking God's listening, huh?"

"He is."

A quick flash of anger distorted his features. "Yeah? Then maybe you should ask Him why we're in a truck with a half-dead guy on our way to visit a drug lord."

"*Silencio,*" Miguel shouted, banging his bat on the metal floor.

Sarah jumped, and Jett leaned against the wall of the truck, bound feet and bound hands.

Bound heart, she found herself thinking, looking at his handsome face, so quick to flash the arrogant smile against the hurt she knew was inside him, a hurt rooted deep in his past. Those brown eyes, the tint of coffee, had sparkled with tears when she'd broken up with him. It was the only time she'd ever seen him close to crying. He'd proudly told her he never cried, even when his father, fueled by alcohol, would get out his wooden stick. No tears from Jett, but she'd cried oceans for him.

His lips were dry, she noticed, and she wanted to ask Miguel for some water, but she knew he wouldn't provide any and Jett wouldn't drink it anyway.

Again she closed her eyes, let the anger and fear settle as best she could, and resumed her prayers. The truck interior was stifling, but the jostling eased off half an hour into the journey. She gathered from the angle of the floor and the grinding of the truck gears that they were headed up a slope, ostensibly toward Beretta's mountain compound.

Facts about Antonio Beretta were mixed with the local storytelling. Depending on the storyteller, he was either the son of a deposed Mexican president or perhaps a farmworker who had taken on the mantle of a drug lord by murdering anyone who got in his way. He provided gifts and favors to certain people, and he also arranged for the abduction and murder of his rivals and their family members. What was the truth? Sarah and Jett were about to find out. She swallowed, a painful motion against her parched throat.

A sudden lurch made her bang the back of her head on the truck's metal siding. She grabbed hold of Young's stretcher to hold it steady as the vehicle bucked and shimmied.

"Flat tire?" Jett suggested to Miguel. "You guys know how to change one? I can show you, if you don't."

She beamed Jett a hard look, which he returned with a lazy smile. She wished he would not antagonize the man with the baseball bat who craved an excuse to beat him senseless.

Miguel said nothing, and the truck rolled to a stop. He marched to the back, reaching for the handle when the door was suddenly rolled up from the outside. Sunlight streamed in, blinding them. Trying to shade her eyes, Sarah caught a glimpse of a gloved hand snatching Miguel out of the truck.

Jett struggled to his knees and crawled to Sarah.

"What's happening?" she breathed.

There was a sound of shouting.

"Don't know. Can you cut me loose?"

She searched her medical bag. "They took my scissors."

"Use something else. Anything sharp. Fast."

She pawed through her bag until a gunshot split the air. Then another.

Jett tensed, leaning close to her. She could feel the

warmth emanating from his body, but it brought her no comfort.

Outside, the noises died away until all Sarah could hear was the sound of her pulse roaring in her ears.

"Who is out there?" she whispered, still searching for something to cut his restraints. She found a small blade in a plastic case. With fumbling fingers, she freed it.

"I can make out two men. Three, maybe."

"The police?" Her heart leaped as she sawed away at the bands around his ankle. "Rodriguez must have figured out what happened and sent help."

Jett stared into the sunlight. "Uh-uh."

Sarah worked frantically with the blade, freeing his ankles. "Jett, what are you thinking? Who are those men?"

"EODs have a motto," he said slowly. "Always Prepare for the Worst."

"How could this situation get any worse?"

Jett put his bound hands on her shoulder and held on, as if he could somehow anchor her there away from the danger. She reached for his hands to try and release them from the zip tie. "Jett?" she asked urgently. "What is it?"

"I don't know, but I've got that feeling."

"What feeling?"

"The kind of feeling I get right before something blows up."

FIVE

Jett waited until his eyes adjusted to the light pouring through the back of the delivery truck.

"Come out," said a figure silhouetted by the sun. The voice spoke in unaccented English—an American as far as he could tell. That was a good sign. Wasn't it? Jett's legs were now freed, but Sarah had not had time to cut loose his wrists.

"Stay behind me," he said to her as he climbed out of the truck. She followed, and he offered his bound hands to help her.

They were on a remote stretch of dusty road, hemmed in on all sides by immense trees, thick as living walls. The shadows and the incendiary temperature indicated it was late afternoon. Jett exhaled in deep satisfaction as he took in the sight of Miguel lying on his stomach, hands bound behind him. A man wearing fatigues kept Alex at gunpoint while another forced him to his knees and tied his hands, as well. Alex's other man was not visible, but presumably had been dealt with, too. Out of the frying pan...

"My name is Tom," said the man who was clearly in charge. Jett could see now that he had crew-cut blond hair. He was shorter than Jett by a good six inches, but strong, tough, with a military bearing. Jett figured him to be in his late forties. "Are you hurt?" Tom inquired, his tone polite, cold.

Sarah shook her head. "But there's a man inside the truck. His name is Del Young. He's gravely injured and he needs to be taken to a hospital right away."

"We are aware, ma'am." In fact, one of their rescuers had already hopped into the back of the truck and was checking Young's pulse.

"Who sent you?" Jett said.

Tom didn't answer. Instead he spoke into a radio unclipped from his belt. "Ready."

Was he radioing another vehicle?

Sarah hugged herself. "Thank you for rescuing us. They were taking us to Antonio Beretta's compound. He is desperate to get his hands on Mr. Young."

"We are aware of that, too."

Sarah blinked in surprise. "How did you know that?"

Tom did not reply.

"So you're well informed," Jett said, "but I didn't get an answer to the question. Who sent you?"

"Does it matter?" Tom said, flat blue eyes fixed on Jett. "You would have been executed shortly when Beretta got what he wanted."

"I like to know who I'm dealing with."

Tom kept his gaze on Jett and Sarah as he bent to listen to a whispered report from the man who had been tending to Del Young.

Sarah tucked her fingers against the small of Jett's back, thumb through the belt loop of his jeans. The gesture touched him. It was the way she'd kept him close when they'd been in crowds in the long-ago days when she'd loved him.

Don't you know I'd never let you get lost? he'd said.

And he wouldn't. At the tender age of eighteen, he would have sacrificed anything to keep her from harm. Back then, he hadn't known that love could end so abruptly, like an exploding mortar. He saw her body had relaxed; she leaned her head against his arm, sagging in relief. He wished he could feel the same.

"I can't believe they found us in time."

"Yeah."

She caught the tone, raising her eyes to his. "What's wrong? They're friendly, aren't they?" she whispered.

He stared at Tom. Friendly? There was no flicker in the blue eyes, no sign of tension in the muscled frame, only complete focus on his mission.

Understandable. Jett was the same when he'd been active duty. The mission came first. Time for chitchat later. A wise strategy when your job was detonating bombs. Still, there was something, a piece that did not fit. One thing he'd learned as an EOD was to trust his instincts.

Tom spoke into the radio, and two vehicles approached from somewhere down the road, where they must have been idling. The first was a battered Jeep. Behind that was a pickup with the back covered by a camper shell. "Please take a seat in the Jeep," Tom said.

Sarah eyed the small vehicle. "What about Mr. Young?"

"He will be transported in the truck." Tom's mouth crimped in a humorless smile. "Don't worry. It's a short drive, and you will all arrive at the same location."

"Which is?" Jett demanded.

Tom didn't answer at first. "You don't trust me?"

"I can count the number of people I trust on two fingers. You're not one of them."

Sarah stood stiffly before Tom. "I demand to be taken to the nearest police station," Sarah said. "We need to contact the American embassy immediately."

"Of course," Tom said. "Please get into the Jeep and we'll depart."

Sarah hesitated, her troubled gaze shifting from Tom to Jett.

Tom held up a palm. "The longer we stay here, the more likely Beretta will send others."

Sarah did not look completely convinced, but she walked to the Jeep and Jett followed behind.

"What about Alex and his men?" Sarah pointed. "What will happen to them?"

"They will be delivered to the police."

"Beretta will kill you," Alex shouted. "He will not let this betrayal go unpunished. You won't live through the night."

Tom did not look at them, but a slight gesture sent his men into motion, taping Alex's mouth and loading him and Miguel into the truck.

"Where's the third one?" Jett asked.

Tom's mouth tightened. "He was able to escape, in spite of his gunshot wound. It's another excellent reason for us to move quickly, in case he survives long enough to inform Beretta."

The driver directed Jett to sit in the front. Sarah was ordered into the back next to another of Tom's men.

"As a precaution," Tom said. "In case Beretta has more of his people on the road. Mr. Jett can keep a lookout from the front seat."

"I'd be more help without my hands bound," Jett said, holding up his wrists.

A moment passed between them, and in that couple of seconds Jett knew.

Jett kept his features composed as Tom removed a knife from a sheath on his belt and considered. Tom lingered there a moment, the blade gleaming in the failing sunlight. He flicked it ever so subtly in Sarah's direction. It was a movement so small only Jett saw it, but he deciphered the unspoken message.

"Be careful, Mr. Jett," Tom said softly as he sliced through the ties. "Dangerous territory ahead."

Tension crackled through his nerves. Dicey situations didn't bother him. Forcing Sarah into a dangerous path was another thing entirely. He knew without question that Tom had an agenda entirely apart from merely rescuing three Americans.

Patience, he told himself. *For now, you and Sarah are safe.*

The Jeep rolled smoothly into a neat U-turn before the driver took off in the direction from which he had come.

Jett caught Sarah in the rearview mirror. She was scared, he knew, but outwardly composed. The glimmer in her iridescent eyes told the story. She also had gleaned the truth.

This was not a rescue. It was another abduction.

Sarah's back ached from the endless drive over dozens of potholes. She'd learned to live with a low level of chronic pain after her car accident, but the rough Mexican roads made every nerve along her spine complain. It seemed to her they were driving in circles, though she was no longer certain even what town they were passing. The sun was setting when they reached an unfamiliar industrial area. They passed a few ramshackle buildings with rusted equipment parked outside and what looked to be an abandoned car. Not one person was visible anywhere, not a single employee or foreman. It was too late for the afternoon siesta. Closed up for the day?

She tried to force normal breathing, but her body was on high alert. These so-called rescuers had their own goals, and she knew it did not bode well for the three of them. *Think, Sarah*, she told herself. *How can you help?* Her medical bag was presumably still in the truck, but she'd stowed the blade that she'd used to cut Jett's ankle restraints in her pocket. It was probably of no use whatsoever, but at least it might give her a chance to help them later on. The guard next to her was not disposed to letting his attention wander, so the tiny knife would have to stay hidden for the moment. *Think like a detective, why don't you? Figure out where you are.*

There was no scent of the ocean in the air, no cooling breeze to indicate they'd moved toward the coast. Inland, she decided. She saw from the position of the sun that they had been traveling north. A town in Tijuana, perhaps?

But why bring them here? Surely a missionary nurse and a dive boat captain would be of little interest or value to anyone. Del Young—he was another story. His sly wink reminded her that he was not the innocent victim he seemed to be. Certainly Antonio Beretta had gone to great lengths to get his hands on Young, and now it appeared there was another interested party.

They pulled to a stop in front of a rusted warehouse. A scarred sign on the front identified it as an import-export business. The man in the backseat got out and rolled up a metal door, the groan of steel loud in the stillness. Her heart pounded as the Jeep pulled forward into the dark interior. The smell of rust and sawdust permeated the air. Rows of stacked pallets crowded the periphery of the otherwise empty warehouse. A nice, quiet, isolated spot in which to murder three Americans. Her breathing hitched. But they could easily have done their killing back in the woods...unless they wanted the bodies to remain undiscovered for a while. The other truck crowded in behind them.

Sarah's guard lowered the door again. It clanked to the ground, vibrating the floor and swallowing them up in darkness. She felt a surge of panic as the darkness closed in, but Tom clicked on a bare overhead bulb that shed a sickly light over the space.

She and Jett got out of the Jeep. She searched Jett's face. He did not appear scared, only angry. That set off little alarm bells inside her. Dominic Jett did not react well to being cornered. In their high school days, they'd gone on a day trip to Los Angeles, where two guys had tried to steal her purse. They'd been lucky to get away with bloody noses. Now Jett stood with his feet apart, hands braced in front of him, eyes flicking the space from man to man, assessing.

In her mind, they had no chance of escape. *Don't try anything, Jett. Please.*

"What now?" Jett snapped at Tom. "Are you ready to tell us what you really want?"

Tom turned to the two who were pulling Del Young from the truck. "Strap him to the stretcher securely. The first part is vertical."

"The first part of what?" Sarah said.

He glanced at her as if he had just now remembered her presence. "The journey."

"The journey where?" she nearly shrieked. "Where are you taking us?"

Tom smiled. "Back home. To the United States."

It was not the answer she'd expected, and it left her dumb with surprise. He was returning them to the US? Had she been wrong about Tom and his colleagues?

Jett snorted. "I don't see a border crossing anywhere around here."

"There are many ways to cross the border."

"Why not do it the easy way?" Jett countered. "We're Americans. Drive us to the border. Turn us over to the authorities, and they'll investigate. We'll get home eventually."

"Eventually is not quick enough. We have a prearranged meeting."

The truth was starting to trickle out. "With whom?" she asked.

"You'll find out soon enough."

Jett strode forward abruptly. The man behind him stepped up, immediately pressing a gun into Sarah's temple. The circle of cold metal dug into her skin, and her heart stuttered into an irregular rhythm. One quiver of his finger and she would be dead. It was terrifying and surreal. Her brain did not believe it, but her flesh went cold.

"Don't," Jett snarled. "Don't touch her."

"There will be no need for violence," Tom said calmly, "if you cooperate and do as you're told. You are navy, aren't you?" A tone of mockery crept into his voice. "You should be well versed in taking orders."

Jett's eyes glittered as he looked from the man holding the gun to Sarah. The muscles in his arms were tensed, every sinew rigid, his body a coiled spring.

She locked on his stare. "It's okay," she said firmly. "We aren't going to resist. We will do as you say and he won't hurt me. Right, Jett?"

His eyes narrowed, wheels no doubt turning as he calculated the chances of knocking the guy with the gun away from her. He could do it—she'd seen him practicing in the ring with a mixed martial arts instructor back in their dating days. But the other three men stood at a careful distance, hands on their weapons, watching. They would not get close until they had to.

Jett would die. The thought made her stomach tie itself into knots. Her former love, her lost best friend—she could not stand the thought of watching him cut down in front of her eyes. For her.

"Right, Jett?" she repeated softly. "This man is not going to hurt me."

Though he did not completely remove the gun, her guard moved it away from her head. His conciliatory gesture to avoid bloodshed, which must have been part of his orders.

After a moment of hesitation, Jett recoiled a fraction, just enough. Sarah's knees went weak with relief, but she held herself steady. If he could be strong, so could she.

"All right," Tom said. "Now that we are clear, it's time to go."

Where? Sarah wondered, her mouth too dry to say it aloud. Jett went to her and took her cold hands in his. He gave her fingers a squeeze, and she squeezed back. The skin on his wrists was raw where he'd chafed against the restraints. She wished she could soothe the angry wounds, but he would not take comfort from her. Blinking back tears of relief, she waited to see what on earth would happen next. Together, they watched.

Tom went to a stack of pallets and he and another man pushed it away. He leaned to the floor, tracing his fingers along the filthy concrete until he found a small divot, which he used as a handle to heave a neatly cut section of the cement upward. It swiveled open on invisible hinges.

"Drug runners are resourceful, aren't they?" Tom said with a smirk.

"This is a drug runner's tunnel?"

Tom nodded. "One of the more sophisticated. Gets the product right into the States without the need for any border crossings or security checks."

Sarah gaped as the men started down a sturdy wooden ladder, carrying Del Young on his stretcher. In moments, they had disappeared deep into the vertical tunnel.

Tom gave a formal bow. "After you," he said.

Dread surged through her body, and for a brief moment she did not think she could get her legs to take her into that dark place. One look at Tom convinced her that if force was necessary, he would not hesitate. Swallowing her fear, Sarah made her body obey.

For the second time that day, she found herself climbing down a ladder, wondering if she was heading toward escape—or a dead end.

SIX

Jett had to agree with Tom on one point. Drug runners were resourceful. The tunnel was neatly hewn, equipped with electricity and some sort of ventilation system. Under their feet were a pair of rails that stretched away into the darkness, designed to efficiently carry their illicit cargo. "I'm afraid we only have transportation for the patient," Tom said as one of his men turned on a small motorized cart. Del's stretcher was loaded inside, along with one man to operate the vehicle.

Sarah insisted on checking him before they took off. "His pulse is steady, but he's going to need more fluids soon. Do you have a blanket? It's cool down here."

The cool felt blissful to Jett, but he realized a badly battered victim had to ward off shock. Tom removed his jacket and draped it over Young. The move revealed his muscled torso and a holster fitted with a Glock. Jett had no doubt the guy had more weapons in his pack and perhaps in an ankle holster.

"Get moving," Tom ordered. "I want to be on US soil by nightfall."

It was one point in their favor, Jett figured. No matter the circumstances, they had to be in a better position to escape once they'd returned to the United States, but he was still not convinced Tom wouldn't kill them before they reached their destination. *Know your enemy*, Marco would have said, but Tom remained an enigma.

The cart took off with its patient loaded aboard.

"Now we walk behind," Tom ordered.

Jett didn't budge. "Water first."

Tom raised an eyebrow at Jett. "Move."

Jett shook his head. "Sarah needs water. Your man there has some in his pack. I saw it."

"And what makes you think he should share?"

"Because you want us alive for some reason, or we'd be dead already. If we're going to keep up a good pace, we need hydration."

Tom's eyes narrowed, but he flicked his head toward his man, who reached for a bottle of water.

Tom stopped him, as if a thought had suddenly occurred to him, removing a flask of water from his own pack. "Here. You may have mine."

Jett forced it into Sarah's hands. "Drink and don't argue."

She sighed and took three deep swallows. He admired the delicate muscles of her neck as she drank, the way her eyelashes fluttered in pleasure. As he stood before her, she took another sip. His back was to Tom as he mouthed "blade" to her. She blinked, made a show of wiping her lips with the back of her hand and coughing as she removed the blade from her pocket and passed it to him with the flask.

He gulped down the rest of the water and handed the empty flask to Tom, concealing the blade in his palm. "Better," he said. "Let's go."

He took off down the tunnel a few steps ahead. Tom hastened to catch up, which didn't give Jett time to do much, so he slid the blade into his front pocket. It was a pitiful weapon, but it might give him an edge against his opponent, who believed them unarmed. Tom took a position right next to Jett, and Sarah was escorted by one of Tom's men.

More patience was required.

"So who paid you to get us away from Beretta?"

"Not your business."

"I think it is."

"And you're not going to shut up until I answer, are you?"

Jett flashed him a cocky grin. "How'd you guess?"

Tom huffed out a breath. "My boss and Mr. Beretta are at odds. He wishes to speak with Del Young about a certain piece of property in Mr. Young's possession."

Jett felt a pounding in his temples. "And Beretta's after the same piece of property? What is it? A drug shipment? Diamonds?"

Tom didn't answer. Jett began to sweat in spite of the chill air. The tunnel sloped upward, and Jett stumbled. He stopped, head down as the floor lurched under his feet. Prickles of alarm rose up along his spine.

He heard a soft cry. Whirling, he saw Sarah crumple, her guard catching her before she hit the floor.

"Sarah!" He lunged for her, but the tunnel was now spinning in front of his eyes. He went down onto one knee. "What...did you do?"

Tom kicked him sharply between the shoulder blades. Jett tried to stop himself from falling, but his body would not obey and he went chest down, the breath whooshing out of his lungs. Through a dizzying haze, he saw Tom lean over and remove the blade from his pocket.

"It would have been easier if you'd just cooperated, but I can't allow a delay. Not that I'd have let you get the drop on me anyway."

The water from Tom's flask. Drugged. Why hadn't he suspected?

He saw Sarah draped over her guard's shoulder, limp and small.

He had to get to her, had to.

His head flooded with memories of his father, a big man, with a stubbled chin and six feet to his credit staggering home from the bar, angry over some perceived mistreatment from his boss, spoiling for someone to beat. Jett offered himself, goading his father into using him for a punching bag, diverting the anger from his mother. The tide of rage swept through him, the sensation of being powerless choking him. He would not succumb.

Got to get to Sarah. He made it to his feet, aiming an uppercut at Tom, which he easily dodged.

"It's no use, Jett. I told you. You're not going to win."

Yes, I am. But his eyes closed anyway, and he slipped into blackness.

A fine mist on her face awakened Sarah. Her senses were numb and sluggish, eyes gritty and mouth dry as dust. It took her a moment to discern that the rolling motion was not her dizzied nerves but wave action. Waves? Her pulse quickened. She'd thought they were going to be loaded on a truck or van. Now here she was on a boat, lying on her back on a bench seat, Young on the other, unconscious. Maybe Tom had been lying about taking them back to the US.

Jett. Where was Jett? She jerked to a sitting position so fast it sent her head spinning. Her heart pounded. Had they left him behind in the tunnel? Or worse? She saw a figure lying on the floor between the two bunks. Jett.

He was very still. She scrambled off the seat and knelt

next to him, fingers searching for a pulse, noting they'd bound his hands again. Through her terror, she felt it, his slow steady heartbeat. She stroked her hands over his cheeks to see if she could rouse him. Her relieved exhale caused Young's eyes to open.

"Where are we?" Young croaked.

She forced the words over her dry tongue. "In a boat. I don't know where we're going."

He sighed. "I do. Now it's all over."

"Where?" she demanded. "And what did you do to make so many people desperate to get their hands on you?"

He pinched his eyes closed and groaned.

"Tell me," Sarah said. "Maybe I can figure a way out of this if you give me some information."

"I took her."

"Who?"

He winced as if in pain. "You're a detective—you have to find her."

The boat began to shimmy, and she clung to the bench seat with one hand, steadying Jett with the other. Her patience began to ebb away. "I don't have to do anything. Whatever you've done, you are going to have to fix it unless you tell me the truth."

"No," Young moaned. She saw sweat on his brow. He was probably feverish.

"Yes," she hissed. "Return whatever or whomever you've stolen before someone kills us."

"I can't."

"Why not?"

"Because I can't remember where she is."

The boat stopped with a jerk that sent Sarah sprawling backward, until her hip banged into a hard wooden beam. She blinked back tears of pain. Tom appeared, and Young hastily shut his eyes.

Sarah did not have time to puzzle over what he had said.

"Where are we?"

"Southern California. The Channel Islands, a privately owned one," Tom said.

The Channel Islands? Her heart surged. Could they really be back in the United States? "Owned by whom?"

"I'll let him do the introductions." He gestured toward the deck. "Please. Come with me. I'm sure you'd like to freshen up."

"I'm not leaving here without Jett."

Tom looked at Jett. "I suppose you're right." He opened a box on the desk, removed a syringe, and before Sarah could stop him, he'd plunged it into Jett's bicep. Jett came to life with a gasp, muscles jerking, eyes wide. He sat up, sides heaving.

"You were drugged. You're okay now," she said, forcing him to look at her.

"You hurt?" he gasped, voice gravelly.

"No."

"Where…?"

She didn't get a chance to tell him as Tom grabbed Jett's bound wrists and heaved him to his feet. They were ushered outside into the starlit night. The air was balmy, salt scented, as they trailed along a dock toward a crescent of rocky beach. Above them a set of cliffs towered, like a giant serpent rising from the sea. Fog obscured much of the lower regions, making it impossible to tell how large the island was. She scanned the horizon, hoping to spot the mainland, which would give her an indication of whether or not Tom had been telling the truth about their destination, but the conditions prevented it.

She and Jett followed a black-clad guide, Tom bringing up the rear. Sarah heard other men rolling a stretcher down the dock, presumably to retrieve Del Young. She was disoriented, hungry, aching. How many hours had it been since they fled the clinic? It was probably somewhere in the very early hours of Thursday morning.

She thought of her sisters. Candace, her oldest sister, called her cell faithfully every Friday. Hope flickered inside her. When Candace received no answer, she would start an all-out investigation. She could picture the determined Candace, curly hair held back in a ponytail, manning the phones with Marco, the man who had kept the office running after their father was killed.

Candace, Marco and her two other sisters would leave no stone unturned to find Sarah and Jett once they found out about the abduction.

Okay, Sarah. It's not much, but it's something.

And just then, it was all they had.

They were loaded into a golf cart–type vehicle and driven along a narrow road cut into the black rock cliffs of the island. Jett figured the temperature must be in the midsixties, but he was cold, sluggish from whatever drugs he'd been given, and his mouth was dry as an old sock. Sarah, too, looked hollow eyed, and he noticed she was shivering. He slid closer to her and looped his tied hands around her shoulders.

She leaned into him.

"Get back," Tom ordered from the front seat.

"She's cold," he snarled. "If you want me to move away, you're gonna have to stop the cart and toss me out."

Tom glared but did not make any move to order the driver to stop. Nor did he take his eyes off them.

Sarah was stiff in his arms, rigid with fear or maybe because of his close proximity.

"Just trying to warm you up," he said. She felt so small, like some of her had evaporated since their high school days, when he'd held her every chance he'd got.

She put her mouth to his ear, lips tickling. "What do you think they want?"

"Uncertain," he said, "but we'll get out of here, I promise."

Promises? He was making promises now? Why would he do that in light of the present situation? It was more a matter of the past, he realized. He'd let her down so profoundly, so cruelly, using his pain to fuel his own reckless behavior. Now that he was so close to her, he wanted desperately to make it up to her, to once again stand tall in her eyes and maybe in his own.

But there was no going back, he knew. She didn't want his help. She was accepting it because there was no one else handy. Somehow Dominic Jett had wound up her only potential rescuer.

She let out a sigh and rested her forehead on his chest for a moment. He experienced a combination of pleasure and pain. He wanted to snuggle her closer, clasp her tight enough to make her believe they would survive, that he was strong enough to see them through.

Then she straightened in his arms, and he let her go.

He figured she was praying.

Probably praying that she would be rescued from this island and delivered safely from him. *Good idea. You and I were never a good fit, Sarah*, he thought, disentangling himself from her. Even if it had been the happiest time in his life.

Head in the game, Jett.

SEVEN

Jett scanned the fog-covered island. The ground was rocky, that much he could tell. How far to the mainland? To help? He could swim a long way if properly motivated, and he was feeling more motivated every moment with Tom's arrogant stare fixed on him.

He would have thought the island was uninhabited, part of the Channel Islands National Park, a chain of eight small islands off the Southern California coast, where he'd done some kelp forest diving in his younger days, enjoyed some abalone and lobster hunts. That opinion changed as they drove down a steep slope, passing a helicopter pad and turning onto a paved road. Another two miles down and they came to a palatial home, softly lit by ground lights. It was a long, rectangular structure, three stories with a pillared front entryway. It had a mausoleum quality to it, but what did Jett know about mansions? He'd lived in a beat-up Dodge truck when he'd had to.

The cart pulled around to what Jett figured must be the back entrance. Tom turned. "You will be permitted to use the facilities. You will be fed. If you try anything stupid like escaping, you will be shot." Tom spoke calmly. "You understand there is nowhere for you to go. This is an island, accessible only by boat or helicopter, neither of which you have at your disposal."

Jett's grip tightened around Sarah's shoulders. "When exactly do we stop with all the cloak-and-dagger stuff and find out about our mystery abductor?"

"Soon," Tom said, and Jett didn't like the smirk. "You'll find out soon enough who you're dealing with."

"We've had a very long day," Jett snapped.

Tom stopped at the top of a staircase and motioned for them to go down. "It's going to get longer." He grinned as they passed him.

When they reached the bottom, they made their way down a long, tiled corridor, which led to the empty kitchen and a final set of stairs.

Jett tried again. "We're not sheep. We deserve to know where we're going."

"All right," Tom said, as he motioned for his partner to unlock a metal door. The smell hit him first, the scent of old stone and mildew, the smell of prison. Time to take action.

Jett spun and clipped the guy on the side of the head with a fist. He went down easily. As Jett lunged for the fallen guard's gun and turned, he realized his opponent had predicted the action.

Tom had his gun drawn, pointed at them both. "That got you nothing. Now get inside or I'll shoot you where you stand."

Jett held up his hands and let out a breath. The guard he'd clobbered shakily got to his feet. They were guided inside a massive wine cellar. He could make out a wall covered with tiny cubbyholes, many of which housed dusty bottles. Electric lights were fixed into pockets in the rock. The low ceiling was formed of honey-colored stone, and he had to hunker down in order to keep from bashing his head on a brick archway.

Ahead, two stone cells faced each other with iron bars across the openings, sturdy bars with shiny new padlocks hanging from the old iron locks. Whoever this nut was, he intended to cage them like animals. Anger flooded past the fatigue. Jett considered trying to overpower Tom again, but he had taken a spot just behind Sarah, shielding himself. *Coward.*

Think it through, he remembered Marco saying time and time again. *Before you blow the fuse.*

He forced himself to breathe.

"Into the cell," Tom said, giving him a shove in the small of the back, which nearly pitched him forward onto his face on the stone floor. Tom clanged the door closed. The padlock clicked into place and the darkness washed over him. The combination of darkness and cold triggered a memory from his arduous fifty-one weeks of navy EOD training. He was a new recruit again, deep at the bottom of the pitch-black training pool. His instructor clipped him on the side of the head, stripped him of his air tanks and left him to find his way, blind and disoriented, back to the surface. He'd felt fear then until he'd reoriented, eventually rescuing himself so he could go on to be an EOD and rescue others. He still felt the weight of that crab pinned to his uniform, the nickname for the coveted badge with its lightning bolts, bomb and shield he'd earned with blood, sweat and tears, the badge he could no longer wear.

"You'll be sent for," Tom was saying.

"When?"

"When you're needed," Tom said. "In the meantime, make yourself comfortable. You're going to be here awhile."

To Jett's surprise, Tom gestured for Sarah to follow him back the way they'd come from.

"Where are you taking her?" he demanded.

Tom didn't answer.

"I said, where you are taking her?" he shouted, smacking a fist against the bars that caged him.

There was no answer except a soft laugh and total darkness as Tom snapped off the light and led Sarah away.

The helplessness and rage filled him, making him want to lash out and kick at the bars with all his might. But one thing he'd learned as an EOD was patience. Slow deliberation meant success, though his emotions tugged at him like a vicious riptide. He would solve the problem, disarm the situation. He forced a couple of deep breaths in and out. Sarah would probably be praying at this moment.

She could go ahead and say her useless prayers, but he was going to do what he always did—give it his all. For himself, and for her.

Settling back into the darkness, Jett began to take stock.

Sarah's pulse thudded in her throat as she was taken up two flights of stairs. Her thoughts circled around Jett. He was probably safest locked up. Maybe she would have a chance to calmly reason with their new abductor. Whoever it was had to be more reasonable than Antonio Beretta. Jett wasn't in the frame of mind for anything calm, so the tact would have to be left to her. Tom ushered her into a bedroom.

"You can clean up in here. The housekeeper put out some clothes. You have five minutes."

"But I—" He closed the door in her face. The room

was large, decorated in white with touches of pink, clearly a woman's room, she thought. On the delicate bedspread was a pair of jeans and a UCLA sweatshirt. She didn't want to wear these things—clearly they belonged to whoever owned the room—but her own clothes were soiled and damp. Quickly she stripped off her pants and pulled on the others. The jeans were too big, so she rolled them up at the bottoms, but there was nothing she could do about the baggy waist. The sweatshirt was also made for a bigger woman, but the soft, dry fleece was bliss against her skin. The bathroom mirror shocked her with her own reflection. Shadows smudged her eyes, and her cheek was scratched. Smears of dirt streaked her chin and temples. She looked like she felt—a scared, frightened child.

The familiar sick sensation, the hopeless, helpless wave, rippled through her insides like it had done in the four long weeks of hospital recovery time. Every time she'd battled her way to consciousness, the emotional maelstrom hit her and pushed her back under when she'd realized that she was not dreaming: her father really was dead. Worse yet, she had been the one at the wheel. At those moments she wanted to slip back into oblivion and keep the terrible truth away. Only God had gotten her through. With His help and the tireless support of her sisters, mother and Marco, she'd gotten her life back, or at least her new version of life. She wasn't going to let it go.

"Sarah," she said to her reflection. "You are not powerless." Quickly she splashed water on her face and rubbed it clean, retied her ponytail, used the facilities and washed her hands. Soap. Water. Dry towels. Strange how just those few meager normalities made her feel braver. The cracked face on her watch told her she still had a few minutes left, so she riffled through all the bathroom drawers for something she could use—scissors, a nail file. They were empty and pristinely clean.

Her search of the dresser drawers also yielded nothing. On the bedside table she noticed an old rotary phone, the kind her mother still kept in the study at home. Hope surging, she snatched it up, until she realized there was no dial tone. She plunked the receiver down. For all its prettiness and the tasteful spring landscapes on the walls, the room had an abandoned feel, as if the occupant had moved out long ago. Not surprising if the lord of the manor made it a policy of kidnapping people, she thought.

Tom must have been keeping time, because he unlocked the door at exactly five minutes by her watch.

"Come on," he said.

She was led down a tiled hallway. A half dozen paintings hung in alcoves along the way, each enhanced by its own soft light. Thundering seascapes, portraits and a handful of abstracts. Sarah was not an art expert by any means, but the work was eye-catching and expensively framed. They passed another room, clearly a gallery, with plush carpet and more framed pieces on the walls.

"You work for an art collector?" she said to Tom. He didn't answer, but she figured she'd been on the mark. On the way, she memorized the floor plan as best she could.

He led her into a formal dining room featuring a long, gleaming wood table. Jett was seated in one of the upholstered chairs, looking out of place.

"Sarah," he said, half getting to his feet until Tom gestured him back down with his gun. Jett's hands were still tied and he had not been allowed a change of clothes. His face was as bruised and tired as hers, though the edge of defiance was as strong as ever.

Play it cool, she wanted to say.

"Our host is an art collector, Jett," she said. It made her feel stronger to take charge of the conversation.

Jett raised an eyebrow. "Bully for him. Did he drag us all the way here to talk about art?"

"In a manner of speaking," said a voice from the shadows. A well-dressed man, maybe in his late sixties, stepped forward. He wore trousers, a button-up shirt open at the neck, and a heavy-gauge knit sweater. As his gray eyes drifted from Jett to Sarah, he sucked in a breath. His hand went to his throat as if his suit collar was too tight. He stared at her, mouth pursed in a surprised circle, a neatly cut wave of silver hair catching the lamplight.

"Mary," he whispered.

Tom cleared his throat. "Mr. Ellsworth, this is Sarah Gallagher, the nurse who was tending to Del Young in Mexico along with this man, Dominic Jett. We brought them here at your request."

Ellsworth stared at Sarah, and the sustained eye contact made her stomach knot. At last he spoke again. "You are wearing her clothes."

"They were left out for me," Sarah said. "I'm Sarah Gallagher."

His eyes narrowed, seeming to come into focus. "Of course. For a moment…" He waved a hand. "Forgive me, I have not been sleeping well."

Jett's expression grew even warier, she noticed out of the corner of her eye.

"Sarah Gallagher," Ellsworth said in a near whisper. "The missionary nurse."

"Right," she said. "And I want to know why you kidnapped us."

"Yes, of course." He blinked. "Please sit down. You must be hungry."

In fact, she was famished. "No. Answer the question."

He smiled. "So like my Mary. Soft and strong at the same time. I'm Ezra Ellsworth, and this is my home, mine and my daughter Mary's. Her mother—" his lip quivered and he cleared his throat "—her mother, Jane, died some years ago of cancer, though she fought it valiantly."

"I'm sorry for your loss," Sarah said. "But you've not explained a thing. We've been kidnapped, threatened at gunpoint and drugged. We're not going to sit down here and have a nice family dinner with you."

Jett smiled, and it pleased her. Her chin went up another notch. She'd felt so…tentative about everything since her father died. Her own confidence, even if it was a bluff, surprised her.

"I apologize for your mistreatment. It has been a stressful time for me," Ellsworth said, sinking down onto a chair.

"We're a little stressed, too," Jett said. "What with being abducted and all."

Ellsworth ignored him, gaze riveted on Sarah. He pulled out a chair next to him, across from Jett.

"Please, do sit down, Sarah."

Perhaps indulging the man would help. She sat and tried a gentler tone. "Why did you have Tom bring us here, Mr. Ellsworth? You went to a lot of trouble to smuggle us out of Mexico. Why?"

"I need Mr. Young, and you two were his best chance of making it to me alive."

"Why do you need him?"

A ripple of disgust distorted Ellsworth's face. "He knows the whereabouts of my two greatest treasures. I am an art collector, as you said a moment ago. Del Young was working to acquire a painting for me. The piece is entitled *The Red Lady*."

Sarah sifted through the odd bits of conversation she'd had with Young. "He mentioned it, I think."

He jerked. "Yes. Did he tell you where she is?"

"No, he was mostly incoherent, but he rambled something about 'finding her.'"

"No doubt he would. *The Red Lady* is a painting by Dutch master Johannes Vermeer."

Jett looked interested. "The guy who painted *Girl With a Pearl Earring*?"

Both Sarah and Ellsworth stared at him. Who knew Jett was an art connoisseur?

Ellsworth raised a finger in salute to Jett. "Very good. Vermeer was a seventeenth-century Dutch painter, only moderately successful in his lifetime, but now..." Ellsworth's face grew rapt. "Now we can truly appreciate the sharp contours, the accents of color. *The Red Lady* is even more spectacular than *Girl With a Pearl Earring*. Just the color palette alone..."

"Okeydoke," Jett said, holding up his palms. "We got it. *The Red Lady* was painted by Vermeer, which means it's worth what, approximately?"

In spite of his abrupt, cavalier attitude, she knew Jett was goading, probing, trying to gauge if Ellsworth was truly an enemy or if he had the potential to be an ally. He'd always seen people in black-and-white, friends or enemies. She didn't have to wonder which camp she fell into. She'd dumped him. Helping her now was merely moral obligation, not anything more.

"*The Red Lady* is priceless," Ellsworth was saying.

Jett laughed. "Everything's got a price. What did you pay for it?"

He drummed his fingers. "If you must be so crass as to stick a tag on her, she was purchased at an auction for thirty million dollars."

Sarah gaped. Thirty million dollars would build an entire hospital in Playa Del Oro and maybe a fire station, too.

Jett whistled. "That's a tidy sum. So *The Red Lady* is yours?"

Ellsworth hesitated for a fraction of a second. "Yes."

"And the problem is?"

"Someone else believes otherwise."

"Who?"

"The man whom I hired Mr. Young to steal from."

A ripple of cold passed through Sarah's heart as the pieces fell into place. "Wait a minute. You hired Del Young to steal *The Red Lady* from Antonio Beretta? I thought you bought it at the auction."

Ellsworth grunted. "No. She was meant to be mine. Young said he could get her for me. He has…skills in this area, which I have utilized before."

"Hang on." Jett put his hands on the table. "So if you weren't the buyer at the auction, *The Red Lady* never belonged to you, did she?"

"I said she should have been mine, if it weren't for Antonio Beretta. I was on my way to the auction to purchase her, but he prevented it, so I arranged the theft to take back what should rightfully belong to me."

"Uh-huh. What could possibly go wrong with that plan? Stealing from a Mexican drug lord," Jett said with an eye roll.

Ellsworth missed the sarcasm. "The plan went perfectly until Young double-crossed me and fled with both my treasures a little over three months ago."

"What is the other one?" Sarah asked. "What is the second treasure Young stole from you, Mr. Ellsworth? Another painting?"

Ellsworth's eyes went hard as flint. "He took my daughter, Mary."

EIGHT

The room was so silent, the ticking of the ridiculously ornate clock sounded loud. Jett couldn't believe what he'd just heard. The whole mess would make a great TV movie. Seriously. Priceless painting is swiped; daughter of a filthy-rich guy is kidnapped. "Del Young stole the painting *and* abducted your daughter?" He wouldn't have thought the scrawny guy capable of either.

Ellsworth hesitated before he took a sip from a crystal glass Tom placed at his elbow. "He no doubt figured he would take Mary to ensure I wouldn't retaliate for the theft of *The Red Lady*." He sniffed, tapping a finger on the drinking glass. "That was a grave mistake, of course."

"How do you know Young abducted Mary?"

Ellsworth looked at the ceiling as if he was seeing an image of his daughter there. "Mary is a graduate of UCLA. Brilliant. Cultured. Her grandfather was an earl. I own a luxury hotel empire that stretches across the world. No one would dare take her, dare to lay a finger on her, except Del Young."

"What about Antonio Beretta?" Jett put in. "He's not shy about snatching people. How do you know it wasn't him?"

"I tell you, it was Del Young," he snapped, emotion

flaring in his eyes for the first time. "He's a con man. A thief." He pronounced the word as if it were an expletive.

He noticed Sarah was surreptitiously scanning the room, memorizing the layout. *That's my Sarah Gal.*

No, not yours, he corrected himself. *Not anymore.*

Ellsworth sat up straighter. "Mary is an extremely intelligent woman, a political science major and a summa cum laude graduate. If there was a way for her to escape from Mr. Young, she would have found it."

"How long has she been gone?" Sarah asked.

"Three months, like I said. She'd returned here after her graduation, and then one morning I awoke to find her gone."

Jett watched Tom's expression as his boss spoke. Tight, controlled, worried.

"Shortly before Mary disappeared, Young told me he was unable to steal *The Red Lady*, that Beretta's security was too great. Lies, of course. He stole it all right and hid it away. He promised to return my money, but he stalled and stalled. When he figured out I was onto him, he abducted Mary and went into hiding. I sent Tom to find him, and he tracked him back to Playa del Oro, where he was undoubtedly intending to meet with Beretta to return *The Red Lady* for a hefty fee and tell him all about me." Ellsworth glared. "Young got a half million from me to steal the painting after Beretta took *The Red Lady* from under my nose at the auction. He used Mary to prevent me from pursuing him."

"How do you know Young didn't already hand over the painting to Beretta in exchange for a fee and ratting you out?"

"Tom tells me you found Young in the act of being beaten up by Beretta's men. They were sent to convince him to hand it over."

"Or maybe they were punishing him after he returned it for stealing from Beretta in the first place," Sarah put in.

Ellsworth considered. "Beretta is a bloodthirsty savage. Young would be dead already unless he needed him alive."

Jett agreed. Furthermore, it made him think Ellsworth was a man who thought through all angles. The quality made for a great EOD technician, and a dangerous enemy. More dangerous than Beretta? He wasn't sure.

Ellsworth looked at a spot on the ceiling, just above the chandelier. "I believe Young has no intention of giving it to either one of us. The man is without scruples."

Jett bit back the urge to laugh at the hypocrisy. "All right. You're out a painting and a daughter. Call the cops. They are trained to find people. They'll figure out where Mary is."

Ellsworth remained silent.

The silence told Jett all he needed to know about Ellsworth. "But you won't involve the police, because it will come out that you hired Young to steal *The Red Lady* from Beretta and you won't ever get her back."

"She was meant to be mine," he hissed, banging a fist on the table. "They are both mine, and I will have them returned. I have more resources than any police department, and now that I have Mr. Young, I will get what I want quickly."

"So if you're such a big shot and you've got this whole thing nailed down," Jett said, leaning in, "why do you need us?"

Ellsworth set his glass down so forcefully the water sloshed over the rim, soaking his hand and the table. He did not seem to notice. "You are here to take care of

Young, get him well enough so he can divulge the whereabouts of *The Red Lady* and my daughter."

"What will happen to us when that moment arrives?" Sarah said.

"You will be set free, of course," Ellsworth said. His smile did not quite reach his eyes as he delivered the lie.

Ellsworth would have them killed after he laid his hands on his treasures, otherwise he'd land himself in prison for abduction. He and Sarah were on borrowed time. They would live as long as Del Young did.

"This isn't right, Mr. Ellsworth," Sarah said. "Holding us all here against our will. It's wrong and you know it."

That's where Sarah made her mistake, Jett thought. She assumed knowing right from wrong meant Mr. Ellsworth would want to do right. Jett suspected the man knew exactly which choice was morally right, but the fact was he simply didn't care. When would she outgrow that naïveté? *People aren't all going to measure up to the Gallagher standards, Sarah.* The thought left a bitter taste in his mouth.

"I'm not a monster, Sarah," Ellsworth said, reaching out to pat her hand. "I'm a businessman. I want what is mine, that's all."

Jett could imagine the ruthless Antonio Beretta saying the same thing. "And what about Young?" He watched a spasm ripple across Ellsworth's mouth. "What will you do with him after your treasures are returned?"

Ellsworth put the glass carefully on the table and eased it into a position directly in front of him. "I'm afraid Mr. Young will die. That is the only choice."

Sarah got up. "I'm not going to keep him alive so you can kill him."

"What choice do you have, really?" Ellsworth said.

"I can choose not to comply." The light picked up gold

flecks in her hair and a gleam of passion in her eyes. Ferocious and gentle at the same time. Magnificent. He mentally shook himself. They were on the same side purely for survival's sake. *Don't forget it, Jett.*

"Then you will be letting him die anyway, and his death will be on your conscience." Ellsworth glanced at the tiny cross on a chain around her throat, and a sly expression emerged. "You're a missionary, Sarah Gallagher. This God you serve—He won't allow you to let Mr. Young die, will He?" Ellsworth's tone was mocking.

Jett twisted uncomfortably. Those could be his own words, used to taunt Sarah for being something he could not be—trusting, faithful, the very qualities that both attracted and infuriated him. He pushed back his chair.

"But if she doesn't comply, what's your action plan then? You're going to kill us?"

"No," Ellsworth said. "I don't kill. I pay Tom to do that for me."

"What kind of a man does that?" Jett snapped.

He turned his cold gray gaze on Jett. "A man who gets what he wants. That's the kind of man I am, Mr. Jett. Make no mistake about it." His tone was soft, but there was steel threaded through. "Mr. Young has been moved to a makeshift hospital room on the third floor. Ms. Gallagher, you will attend him as you need, escorted by Tom and Mr. Jett, should you need any assistance."

Jett held up his hands. "I can't assist with my hands bound."

Ellsworth smiled. "All right. Cut him loose, Tom."

Jett raised an eyebrow in surprise.

"That's a bad idea," Tom said. "He's already caused trouble."

"That's because he didn't know that the entire house is under camera surveillance."

Jett didn't flinch. Cameras could be beaten. They were just simple machines, like the breadbox-size robotic cameras he'd carried as an EOD, designed to gather intel without exposing a soldier to injury. He'd figure out a way to outsmart the cameras.

"And besides," Ellsworth said, beaming, "Mr. Jett hasn't received our gift yet."

Gift? His gut tightened, but he kept his face expressionless.

Ellsworth took a box from a small drawer in the sideboard, extracting a heavy-duty black band with a small rectangle attached. He smiled. "You lived a difficult life as a teen, didn't you, Mr. Jett? I'm sure some of your acquaintances might have been sporting one of these? Perhaps your father, even, when he was out on one of his probations?"

Jett ground his teeth. Ellsworth had been doing some research.

Sarah peered curiously at the gadget and then at Jett. *Don't let her see you react*, he ordered himself, biting down on the fury.

"What is it?" she asked.

"He knows, don't you, Mr. Jett?" Ellsworth cocked his head, birdlike, looking at Jett out of the corner of his eye. "Tell her."

"It's an electronic monitoring bracelet," Jett said through a clenched jaw. "The kind they put on prisoners under house arrest."

Horror crept into her eyes, dulling the vivid color.

"Very good." Ellsworth handed it to Tom. "We can track your every move." He laughed. "There is nowhere on this island you can run where we will not know about it within moments, Mr. Jett." His laughter sounded high and reedy in the enormous dining room. "So go ahead and cut him loose, Tom. Then put our little gift around his ankle."

It took all of Jett's will to stand docilely by as Tom cut the zip tie that bound his wrists and fastened the tracker around his ankle.

There's nowhere on this island you can run...

He blazed a look at Ellsworth who stood smiling, like a child who'd just received a coveted toy. *Enjoy it now, because soon I'm going to be saying the same thing to you, Ellsworth.*

Nowhere you can run...

Sarah insisted on checking out her patient immediately. She was reassured to find him resting comfortably on a small bed with clean sheets that had been set up for him in an empty bedroom. His pulse was strong and his color good. Basic medical supplies stood in tidy piles on a table. She checked his dressing and got another IV started with Jett's help. Young's eyes flickered open.

"Where?" he asked.

"On Ellsworth's island," Jett said. "And he wants his painting and his daughter back."

Sarah glared at Jett, but Young had already closed his eyes and flopped back onto the pillow. She bent close and whispered in his ear. "We need to talk if you want to stay alive. I'll be back when I can," she said in case he was feigning being unresponsive.

"Come on," Tom called. "You both need some shut-eye. Mr. Ellsworth wants to interrogate Young this afternoon. Rest up until then." He led them back down to the wine cellar.

"What time is it?" Sarah asked.

"Almost ten a.m. on Thursday morning."

"We're hungry," Jett said. "How about some food?"

"Provisions are in your cells."

"Too cold in there."

"There are blankets."

"Not good enough."

Tom opened the cellar door with a jerk. "This isn't a spa vacation, Jett. You're here to do a job, so shut up and do what you're told."

"Is that what you do?" Tom would not meet Jett's eye. "You're just a hired killer who takes orders from some rich guy? He's lying about something, and you're covering up."

That earned Jett a hard shove that sent him headfirst into his cell. Then Tom led Sarah into hers. At least this time he left the lights on when he departed. She saw there was indeed a pile of blankets, a small cot and a tray with fruit, a bottle of water, cheese and bread on it.

Jett cracked open his bottle and drained the entirety in moments. Then he began munching on an apple while he paced the length of his cell. Sarah was too hungry to do much but wrap the blanket around herself and do the same, making her way from apple to cheese and the sliced bread. When she was done, she saw Jett staring at her, fingers curled around the bars.

"Looks like there's a small staff that I've identified from a duty schedule I saw on the wall—the housekeeper, a cook—but he might have sent most of them away. Haven't seen any sign of them. There's Tom and two guards. There must be one guard dedicated to watching my tracking coordinates, unless Tom can do that on his cell phone."

Sarah jumped when something soft glided by her leg. A Siamese cat wound its way around her ankles and she bent to stroke it. "And a cat," she added.

He laughed. "All right. Five humans and one cat.

They've also probably got a helicopter pilot and boat captains on the payroll." He looked at Sarah. "What's Young's status, really? Is he faking being unconscious?" Jett spoke so low she had to strain to hear him. Was he worried there might be listening devices recording their conversation?

"Not at the moment, I don't think, but Jett, there's something you should know."

"I'm all ears."

She recalled the earlier conversation she'd had with Young in the boat on their way to Ellsworth's island. "He said he doesn't remember where he left *The Red Lady* and Mary," she whispered.

"He what?" Jett snapped. "Is he lying to buy time? Save his skin?"

"I'm not sure. He sustained a serious head injury, so it's possible he's telling the truth."

"Or he's lying, knowing that once he gives a location, it's lights-out." Jett thudded a fist against the bars. "I just need to get my hands on a cell phone. One call would do it."

"My sister Candace calls me every Friday. When I don't answer tomorrow, she'll start looking."

He nodded, eyes shifting thoughtfully. "That's something positive, anyway."

"So what should we do now?" Sarah watched as the cat slunk through the bars and disappeared into the shadows.

"Get some sleep."

She knew Jett was a hopeless insomniac even when he wasn't imprisoned. "What are you going to do?"

"Lie here and think."

She giggled.

"What's so funny?"

"You didn't used to value the 'stop and think' method.

Usually you went with the 'do it and repent later' technique."

"Name one time," he said.

"When you decided you knew how to water-ski without any practice and you wound up with two black eyes and a concussion."

"Okay, that's one, but you can't name a second."

"When you challenged Marco to a boxing match on your seventeenth birthday, and it was over in three minutes."

Jett sighed. "That's only because he took it easy on me. It would have been one, but he was trying not to embarrass me too much in front of you."

She remembered that seventeenth birthday for a different reason. She'd baked him cookies—oatmeal raisin, his favorite—and showed up at his house to deliver them. Jett had never invited her over before, so she'd thought she'd leave the cookies on the doorstep to surprise him. The front door was open, a broken beer bottle on the porch. Jett was kneeling at his mother's feet, dabbing at a cut on her arm with a cotton ball.

She'd immediately offered to help, and the startled looks on their faces were ones she'd never forget. His mother's, sorrowful and guilt ridden, and Jett's, anguished and overwhelmed with a rage he quickly concealed. His mother told Sarah that she'd cut herself while framing a picture. Jett stayed stone silent until he'd escorted her outside.

"Jett, is that what really happened?" She'd noticed then in the sunlight that he had a bruise starting to form on his cheekbone.

He'd stared at her then, mouth tight with pain. "We can talk about it later."

Only he never had, and she'd never pushed him to.

"Yeah," Jett said, chuckling through the bars of his cell. "I learned never to challenge Marco to a boxing match. I still wouldn't, even now."

"I liked your impulsive side."

"You did?"

"Sure."

"Your dad didn't."

"He is…" She swallowed. "He was protective."

"True story. He labeled me a loser, and that was as far as he went getting to know me."

"You didn't take the time to let him get to know you, so don't blame my father."

"Not enough time in the world."

Her jaw was tight, shoulders tense, so she tried to let out a breath. No one on the planet infuriated her more than Jett. And no one had the right to criticize her father. "Well, he's dead now, so you're right about that." A wasp sting of grief punctured her once again.

There was silence from Jett's cell. "Hey, um, I forgot for a minute there."

I never forget, she wanted to say. *Not for one moment.* She saw the strong planes of Jett's face, the dark hair, which had begun to grow out of the ever-present crew cut and was now long enough to touch the tops of his ears, the inky-black thatch of hair she'd loved to touch.

"I'm… I mean, I'm sorry about what happened to your dad. He was a quality man, even though he couldn't stand me."

"It wasn't that he didn't like you."

"Funny, I didn't read it like that when he said he never wanted to catch sight of me around you or he'd flatten me."

She sighed. "You gave him plenty of ammo. Drinking. Getting into fights. Dropping out of high school."

"Even if I hadn't, he wouldn't have thought I was good enough for you." Jett's tone was not angry, just sad. "Drunk for a dad. Moving around one step ahead of the repo man. The Jetts were from the opposite side of the tracks than the Gallaghers."

"That's not true."

"Yes, it is." His dark eyes fastened on hers. "And deep down, you thought the same."

"I did not, Jett. Stop putting words into my mouth."

"Sarah, can you look me in the eye and tell me that you didn't think I needed fixing?"

Inside, she burned not with anger, but with shame. It was true. All the while they were dating, she'd thought she understood Jett and his circumstances. Had she truly wanted to understand him? Or just change him?

"That's what I thought," he said when she did not reply. "The Gallaghers and their American dream life."

Shame flipped to anger. "Really, Jett? Is my life really so perfect? I wasn't aware that part of the American dream is having your father murdered." She forced the words past the lump in her throat. "Knowing that someone wanted him dead, and if perhaps I'd been a better driver maybe he wouldn't be. Doesn't feel like the perfect life to me."

A sob escaped her lips, and she clamped them shut.

"Sarah Gal," he said, pressing against the bars. "Hey."

Her vision blurred with unshed tears, and for a moment her body longed to be in his embrace, there in the darkness in this strange place with danger filling every inch of the horribly gorgeous house. But there would be no comfort in his arms ever again. It was just a distant high school memory forged before both their lives had taken drastic turns. "Jett, I don't want to get into this now.

I miss my dad so much sometimes it hurts to breathe. Can we leave it at that?"

"Yeah. I'm sorry. Shoulda kept my big trap shut." He hesitated. "Are you okay? I mean, healed up from your accident? Marco said you came through it like a champ."

She wiped a hand across her eyes. "I have back pain and I lost a lot of weight, but I'm doing better all the time. God's been healing me inside and out."

He didn't answer.

"Marco told us about your accident, Jett. I tried to call many times, but you never answered."

"I know." He cleared his throat. "Ironic thing is I was injured in a training exercise when our vehicle rolled off the road. It wasn't even doing the thing I studied so hard to do. Couldn't even get that right."

"Will you be able to return to EOD someday?"

"No." His gentle tone bottomed out into something hard and flat. "I have occasional seizures, and I lost some vision in my left eye. I'm washed up."

"No, you're not."

He shook his head. "Sarah, I'm glad you got your healing, but God's not doing anything for me, inside or out. The best times in my life are long gone, and no Pollyanna, God-loves-you speech is going to change that."

She heard the ache, the anguish, and she wished she could stretch out her fingers through the bars, even though there was no way she could reach him. She'd never been able to reach that vulnerable place in him. She could only pray that God would. "Jett…"

"Get some sleep while you can." He sprawled onto his cot, big shoulders slumped toward the unforgiving stone wall.

NINE

It was after seven, and they were still locked in their cells. Sarah had gone quiet, finally ending her pacing and lying down on the thin cot. He'd tossed his blanket over to her to add to the one she had, since it was dank and cold in their makeshift prison. She'd refused, he'd insisted, the argument continuing until she'd given up with an exasperated sigh. Better she be aggravated than cold, he figured. He hoped she was sleeping, since she'd not closed her eyes for a moment since they'd been taken from the clinic, except for her drug-induced state during the tunnel episode

Though Jett was lying quietly on his own cot, he was light-years away from sleep. Instead he was trying to figure out a way to ensure an escape route for Sarah. Marco trusted him to take care of her, and this was one mission he was going to complete. Marco had saved Jett's life, and there was no way he was going to let him down.

He could picture his sixteen-year-old self, how awed he'd been that the tough navy SEAL took notice of a skinny, bruised kid, sleeping in his truck and sneaking into the gym to use the shower. All the bluster and tough talk hadn't fooled Marco for a minute. Somehow he'd been able to see through all the bravado and known that

Jett was hurting and desperate, even though Jett refused to give him particulars.

"You decide whether you're gonna make it or not," Marco had rumbled one day when he found Jett trying to jimmy the vending machine into popping out a free candy bar since he hadn't the coins to buy one. Marco pressed a thick finger into Jett's chest. "Not your dad, not your mom, not your circumstances—you." Then Marco had forced a disgusting kale smoothie and twenty dollars into his hand and told him he could bunk on Marco's boat, the *Semper Fortis*, when things got too rough at home. The little boat had become his real home, and Marco more of a father than his own.

And in that instant in front of the vending machine, Jett had known he would never disappoint this man if he could help it. The Gallagher sisters meant the world to Marco, and he'd entrusted Jett with Sarah's safekeeping. The ultimate act of respect from the finest man Jett had ever known. He would not let him, or Sarah, down. Resolve hardening in his chest like quick-drying cement, he forced his thoughts back to possible escape plans.

Ellsworth was so certain that his tracking bracelet would keep him in place—Jett might be able to use that to his advantage. If he caused a ruckus somehow, it might buy time for Sarah to get to a phone, barricade herself in somewhere until help arrived. It wouldn't take much. One phone call or email would be enough to call in the cavalry. He was still mulling over the idea when Tom led them out of the wine cellar up to the main house.

"Did you sleep?" he asked Sarah as they exited the gloomy space, more to insert some normalcy in the bizarre situation than anything else.

She shrugged. "A little. I kept thinking this must be

a bad dream, but when I opened my eyes, nothing had changed. I prayed a lot."

Waste of time, he thought, but instead he quirked a grin. "This is gonna be a great addition to your detective case files when we get out of here."

"You think so?"

"Oh, yeah. It can go under 'Hard-Boiled Detective—Island Abduction.'"

He saw her chin go up slightly and a little spark returned to her eye. *Score one for Jett.*

Tom made them go first, climbing up to the third floor until they made it to the bedroom where Young was kept. He saw Sarah eye the doorway to a small office, probably where the estate's bookkeeping was done, before they reached the bedroom. She too was searching for an opportunity, an escape route of some kind.

Young lay still underneath a crisp white blanket. Sunlight lit the clouds, sending a watery light through the window on the wall across from the bed. It highlighted the ghastly pallor of Young's face, the yellow-green bruises marring his cheeks and temple. The guy looked liked he'd gone a few rounds with a boxing champ and lost. Big-time.

When he heard them enter, he lifted his head.

Sarah went to him and offered a brilliant smile that was probably more powerful than any medicine she could have given him. It reminded Jett of the one she'd given him when he woke up after the motorcycle crash. That smile had stayed with him, lingered in his soul to this day for some reason, which he didn't understand.

"You're awake," Sarah said to her patient. "I'm so glad. How are you feeling?"

He stared at her. "Who are you?"

"Sarah Gallagher, the nurse, remember?"

Was Young truly confused or putting on another act?

Young's gaze darted around the room, finally alighting on Tom. He seemed to momentarily gain focus. "You're Ellsworth's man."

"Of course," Tom snapped. "You know that perfectly well, so drop the act. You're not fooling anyone."

"I'm dying," Young said.

"Not yet," Tom said, "but you're going be soon if you don't tell me what I need to know."

"You want to know where *The Red Lady* is, don't you?" Young whispered, ending in a wet-sounding cough.

"Yeah," Tom said. "Where did you stash her?"

Jett's heart sped up. *Don't tell him. Not yet.* "You're sick," he said. "Let Sarah do her nurse thing first."

Young waved a hand. "I have to tell right now. I think I'm not gonna make it much longer." His eyes burned, spittle catching on his lower lip.

"You're overreacting," Jett said. "You're going to be okay. You just need some time to recover."

"Quiet." Tom pushed Sarah and Jett aside. "There is no more time. I'm listening. Tell me what you did with *The Red Lady*."

"And Mary," Sarah added.

Young looked puzzled—Jett figured his brain wasn't yet firing on all cylinders, but at least the alertness was a good sign, depending on what he revealed. *Don't talk too much, Young*, he willed. *You'll be signing our death warrants and yours, too.*

Young looked at Jett and Sarah, recoiling as if he'd just noticed their presence. "I don't know you two. Get away. This information is for Mr. Ellsworth. I can only tell Ellsworth's people." His skinny legs writhed under the sheets.

Sarah made a placating gesture. "Of course." Shooting

Jett a look, she stepped aside to join him. Instinctively, he took her hands in his. Hers were not satin-soft hands, but slightly rough with hard work and the difficulties they'd faced in the last few hours. She'd never been the prissy type with perfect nails and lotioned skin anyway, and he'd loved her for it. The moment he'd first seen her in the high school gym—hair messy, jeans splattered with paint, holding a dripping paintbrush—he'd thought her more beautiful than any other woman he'd ever laid eyes on. That opinion had never changed.

The sentimental streak puzzled him. Pulling his thoughts away from the past, he squeezed again and gave her a wink.

She offered a slight smile, confident, or so she pretended. Confident when she had no right to be so. She probably expected that God was right in the midst of all this insanity, that He would somehow work the thing out for good, as she'd told him so many times before, but Jett had no such confidence. He was on his own, just like he'd always been, and Sarah was, too, though if she wanted to delude herself, there was nothing he could do about it.

His mind raced as he watched Tom reach for Young. If Young delivered all the info, there would be no reason to keep any of them alive, but he hoped they would have a little time while Ellsworth checked out Young's veracity. Ellsworth hopefully would not take any hasty actions with a thirty-million-dollar painting and his daughter's safety hanging in the balance. He'd keep Young around until the painting was in his greedy hands, then he'd have Tom kill them all. No witnesses, nice and tidy.

A phone was still their best chance. Hope flickered up in his gut when he noticed the telltale outline of a cell in Tom's back pocket as he bent over Young's bedside. It might be their one and only chance.

"All right, you little worm," Tom growled. "Be a man for once in your life and tell me. Where's *The Red Lady?*" Rage mottled his face.

Jett let go of Sarah's hand and took a step closer. Tom was a good fighter, wary and tough, but at the moment he was completely focused on hearing the truth from Young. One hard hit in the back of Tom's neck and Jett could grab the phone, hand it off to Sarah and she could run, hide and get off a hurried phone call. Marco would have the island overrun with cops in no time.

"Get ready," he mouthed to her.

She clutched his arm, shaking her head, telling him no.

It's not the time to argue, he wanted to snap at her.

"Come on," Tom said, grabbing a handful of blanket. "Start talking."

"Don't." Sarah stepped forward and grasped for Tom's arm. "He's injured."

Jett reached to pull her back. She could not be between him and Tom.

Without warning, Young leaped off the bed, sending the blankets flying. He lunged for Tom, grabbing the gun from Tom's holster and throwing an elbow under Tom's chin. The blow landed with a sharp thwack against his throat. With a gagging sound, Tom stumbled back.

"Get away," Young said, gun clutched in his shaking palms. "Get away from me, all of you. I'm getting out of this loony bin."

Jett pulled Sarah behind him.

Tom recovered his balance, quivering with rage. "You don't have the guts to shoot, Young. You're a miserable coward," he shouted. "You always have been."

Young's finger tightened on the trigger. A shot exploded through the room, shattering the lamp next to Sarah's head. Bits of glass rocketed through the air. There was no place for cover in the small room. Jett's blood surged and he shoved her behind a spindly chair as another shot drilled the ceiling, sending bits of plaster flying in all directions. The recoil jerked Young, almost knocking him over, but he kept his balance.

Jett heard the sound of feet pounding up the stairs.

"Reinforcements," Tom yelled at Young, his body in a half crouch, one arm thrust forward as if to ward off any more wild shots. "You're gonna die unless you put the gun down right now."

The guard would make it through in seconds and return fire. There was no way they'd survive being in the middle of a gunfight. Jett threw himself at the door and locked it seconds before the guard's body slammed into the other side.

Hatred simmered in Tom's eyes as he stared at Jett, but he did not dare turn his back on Young in order to unlock the door. The guard began to kick the wood with his booted foot. It was a simple interior door, not suited for such heavy abuse, and it began to shudder immediately. Splinters of wood broke free from the frame. They had minutes, no more.

Sarah was crouched behind the chair, trembling in fear. He knelt next to her, making himself a smaller target for Young, but still big enough to protect Sarah as best he could.

Young's eyes were frantic, searching for an avenue of escape.

He's got no options, Jett thought. Stairs blocked, no way off the island unless he planned on commandeering a boat or helicopter. He was trapped, and there was nothing more dangerous than someone with no options. The guard's booted food rammed through the door. A hand reached through to unlock it.

"I'm not dying here," Young rasped.

Tom took action, leaping forward and grabbing for Young's wrists.

Another shot rang out, and Tom stumbled back, the bullet grazing his shoulder, a trail of red darkening his sleeve. He grunted in pain, but instead of retreating, he sprang toward Young, hands reached out in a stranglehold.

"No," Young screamed.

The guard charged through the wrecked door, Glock gripped in both hands.

"Don't kill him," Tom ordered. "We need him."

But the guard took a shot anyway, the sound deafening as the bullet struck a glass shelf, fracturing it into tiny projectiles that peppered the floor.

Jett again covered Sarah as best he could, feeling sharp bits cutting through the material of his T-shirt. When the shot died away, he dived for the guard before he could loose another shot. They grappled, the gun gripped between them. Jett got the guy in a chokehold, applying as much pressure as he dared.

The guard grunted and gasped, finally letting go of the gun to claw at the arm cutting off his oxygen before he collapsed unconscious onto the floor.

Jett was going for the gun until, with one last panicked shout, Young came to life.

He threw himself against the window at full speed.

The pane shattered with a roar as Young punched through the third-story window.

Through a cascade of tinkling glass, Jett froze in disbelief. He too felt as though he was trapped in a bad dream as Sarah dived forward, grabbing at Young, clutching his legs before they both tumbled out the window.

TEN

The breath was driven out of Sarah. She and Young landed on a narrow ledge outside the window, pieces of glass shooting past them into the air. She hauled him back against her body and kept him from pitching forward, fabric ripping as she gripped his shirt. His heart hammered through the thin material.

"Stop moving," she panted, back pressed against the exterior of the house. "We'll fall."

"I'm not staying here. Let me go." He slapped at her hands, and she felt the ledge underneath her hip shudder. It was purely decorative—not intended to support the weight of two adults.

"Calm down," she commanded in the voice she'd used to soothe dangerously hysterical patients.

"Ellsworth will kill me."

"He won't. We'll save you somehow."

Jett was scrambling through the window now, calling her name. Tom shouted at his man inside.

Young thrashed and wriggled until she was forced to let go of him in order to keep from falling herself. He sat down on the ledge, legs dangling, and gave her a final curious look. "You don't understand, do you?"

"Understand what?"

He shook his head, grabbing her hand with bony fingers. "Get off this island any way you can. Ellsworth doesn't know how to handle losing, and now that he has... he's gone mad."

"Return the painting," she said. "That's all he wants."

Young released her sadly. "No," he said quietly. "That's not all."

"I don't understand."

"Just get away before it's too late." He got to his feet, bits of paint chipping away and floating off into the air.

"Don't..." she called.

But Young had scooted to the edge.

"Wait," she screamed.

He leaped.

Breath caught, Sarah peered over. The sun was low in the sky, but it was not yet fully dark. A precisely trimmed hedge edged the house and yard. She couldn't see him anywhere, until she caught movement and he wriggled out of the shrubs, limping but seemingly unharmed.

Without a backward glance, he staggered away, losing himself in the trees.

Sarah felt strong hands grabbing her arms and she was lifted off the ledge. Jett pulled her clear of the window and eased her to her back on the floor.

"Sarah." His voice was soft, chocolate eyes wide with shock. He brushed the hair from her face. "Are you hurt?"

For a moment they were the same gentle eyes that gazed at her with such love and admiration all those years ago. His mouth, warm and tender, brushed her temple. She wanted to drift away and just feel, remember, relive. *But you'll wake up, Sarah.* Like she woke up every day, thinking for a fleeting second before her brain became fully conscious that her father might actually be alive.

She'd not stopped them from going over the cliff. "No," she said finally. "Not hurt."

He was shaking his head now, anger flickering to life. "That was ridiculous, insane. You could have broken your neck trying to save a no-good criminal."

"He's my patient."

"He's a liar and a thief."

"He's precious to someone." *Like you were precious to me*, she wanted to say. *Even when you were drinking. After you dropped out of high school. When we broke up because you drove too fast and fought too hard and cared too little and you wouldn't change, even for me.* The thoughts hurt more than her banged-up body.

She sat up, his arm supporting her back. "He made it. He was running off the property grounds after he jumped."

"There's nowhere for him to go." Jett grabbed a roll of tape and gauze off the medical cart. Kneeling beside her, he pushed up the leg of her jeans. "Sit still."

Shouting echoed down the hallway through the open door.

Jett cocked his head. "Tom and his colleague mounting a search detail."

"They left without locking us up."

"Didn't have time. Their first priority is Young. It won't take long before they find him."

"We have to help Young before he gets himself killed."

"No, we have to treat this cut."

She looked down to find a ribbon of blood on her shin, which had begun to throb. "I'm okay, Jett. Please, let's go find Young before he gets into worse trouble."

He yanked off the piece of tape and unwrapped a sterile gauze pad. "We're not going to get him out of the hole he's dug for himself. We can't save him."

"We can try."

"Don't you get it?" His eyes flashed dark fire. "We're in this mess because of him. He doesn't deserve our help. We've been abducted and imprisoned because of this joker you feel so sorry for."

"Jett…"

"No, Sarah. This isn't one of your missionary cases. He's a criminal."

"He's scared and he needs help."

"You're not thinking straight. Take off your rose-colored glasses, because our situation is anything but safe right now."

His anger was palpable, a wave that hit her full force. She sucked in a breath and tried to reach for the tape. "I can do that."

He kept it out of her reach. "Try to be the patient, would you? Young's a lost cause. Take off your missionary hat for one red second."

She winced as the bandage chafed against the laceration. "You didn't used to mind my idealism."

He stopped for a minute before he eased her pant leg back down. "This is a different situation."

"We can help him."

"You can't save them all," he said.

She smiled and could not resist tracing a finger over the angry line of his brow. "But I can try."

He caught her palm and brought it against his cheek. "Don't you ever get tired of championing lost causes? Why would you want to keep trying, Sarah Gal?" he said softly.

"God made me that way."

Something shimmered across his face—anger, hurt, disappointment, and maybe deep down a tiny glimmer of hope. He wanted peace, he wanted to experience love and forgiveness, but he was too proud to accept the terms. *God loves you*, she wanted to say. *Let Him give you what you need, even if you don't want it. He's the only way to lose all that anger.*

Jett set the tape and gauze aside and got to his feet, offering her a hand. She rose, blinking against a wave of dizziness. For a moment, she leaned against him and he clasped her around the waist while she rested her head on his shoulder. He laid his cheek on the top of her head. "Oh, Sarah. What am I going to do with you?"

She sighed as the dizziness subsided. The small office they'd seen that was the most logical place to find a phone was locked, so they made their way downstairs.

"The second guard is probably already en route to intercept now that my tracking bracelet indicates I'm moving."

The front door was open, banging due to the wafts of cold air drifting in.

Lights clicked on upstairs, a golden pool illuminating the landing.

"Go search for a phone," he whispered. "If you find one, call for help and hide."

"Where are you going?"

He sighed. "To find your lost sheep."

Her mouth opened in surprise. "Why?"

"Because if I don't, you will."

Her heart danced just a little, and she wrapped her arms around his shoulders. "Dominic Jett, you are a good man."

He rested his cheek on her head, mumbling into her hair. "No, I'm not, Sarah. And we both know it."

Before she could answer, he'd pulled loose from her arms and sprinted out the door.

* * *

Jett headed for the motor noise. Tom gunned a golf cart to life, yelling at his number-two guy.

"He's going for the dock, Cy. Cut him off from the other side. Radio me if he heads for the cliffs."

Cy hopped in another cart, and they took off in different directions.

He wondered if Del Young knew how to handle a boat. The wind had picked up, the clouds covering the rising moon. The smell of rain hung heavy in the starless night. It was only ten miles or so off the coast of Santa Barbara, and if Young could make it to the mainland, he could quickly lose Ellsworth's goons, but it was treacherous going even for a seasoned sailor.

Jett ran along the side of the small gravel road Tom had taken. It felt good to be moving fast and hard, the cold air enveloping him, energizing him. The tracking bracelet was no doubt relaying his coordinates.

That's right, he thought. *Come on after me and leave Sarah alone*. It couldn't take too long for her to find a phone. There had to be one in the kitchen, or the art gallery he'd seen on the ground floor, or the small office. *Hurry, Sarah.*

Tom had a head start, but Jett had the advantage of being able to stray from the gravel road, so he took off, sprinting over the most direct route across the black rock. He kept a good pace, slowing only when the rocks moved under his feet and threatened him with a turned ankle. After a hard ten-minute run, he crested a peak in the rocks that overlooked a slice of cove and the dock.

They'd been brought to the island on a forty-foot boat, which he saw moored in a slip below.

He heard Tom's golf cart approaching and saw the lights from the one the guy named Cy was driving. Jett scrambled down from his rocky perch, peering through the darkness for any sign of Young. What exactly was he supposed to do with the guy when he found him, anyway? Jett figured he'd cross that bridge when he came to it.

With a ping of gravel, Tom screeched into view and slammed to a halt. In seconds he was out, running for the dock toward the big boat. It was well secured, tied to the dock cleats at the bow and stern as well as the spring line in between. It would take several minutes to free it and another to fire the engine to life, provided the ignition key had been left aboard. Tied at the far end of the dock was a motorboat, and Jett guessed that would be Young's choice.

Ducking low, he raced along, the wooden planks slick under his feet. Young was there, all right. He'd just pulled the choke out and twisted the throttle.

"Stop," Jett said. The creep intended to save himself and leave Jett and Sarah to whatever fate Ellsworth would come up with. It made his blood boil.

Young's eyes were so wide they seemed to start from the sockets. Jett was five feet away now and closing fast. Young twisted the throttle again.

"I said stop," Jett shouted, adrenaline roaring through his veins.

Young pulled the cord, and the motor sputtered to life. He cast off the line.

Three feet.

The boat pulled free.

Another foot to go.

The propeller churned in the water. Young did not look back, shoulders hunched as if he was willing the boat to go faster.

Jett neared the end of the dock. Decision time. Stop and hope Tom could catch him in the larger boat.

Or go.

For Jett, it was go time. He accelerated, launched himself into the air and jumped.

He slammed against the corner of the stern, inches away from the thrumming motor. The vessel was picking up speed, the vibrations threatening to shake him loose. He clamped his fingers around a cleat and hung on.

Young was not an accomplished boater, and their path was erratic as he headed out into the open sea.

Muscles bunched, Jett got a leg over the gunwale and heaved himself aboard.

The action surprised Young, who yelped, grabbing an oar and swinging it toward Jett's head. He deflected with his forearm, letting Young's momentum carry him forward until he fell on his knees on the deck.

Jett was on him then, knees on his back, securing his arms behind him and reaching to turn off the motor with the other.

"We can get away," Young panted, cheek mashed against the deck.

"And leave Sarah behind? When she's done nothing but try to keep you alive? You're a real hero, huh?" Jett shook the water out of his face.

"I never wanted to be a hero. I just wanted to have enough to get along in the world, you know? A piece of what everyone else has."

"You can't get your piece at someone else's expense. It doesn't work that way. It's too late. We're going back."

Young shook his head, tears glinting in his eyes. "He's crazy. Sure, the whole thing started out as a con, a way to get close to Ellsworth's art, but things changed. I loved Mary, loved her so much, and for some reason she loved me, too. I didn't deserve it."

Young's words sank into Jett's heart. *I didn't deserve*

it. How much worry he'd put Sarah through with every fight he'd gotten entangled in, every time he'd chosen to drink and party in a desperate attempt to belong. He clamped down on any sympathetic feelings. Now wasn't the time or the place to hear Del Young's side of the story. He was the reason they were in this mess in the first place. "You got a funny way of showing love, conning her father."

"Ellsworth is crazy. Certifiable. That's why we can't go back."

"I'm not going to leave Sarah," he blazed at Young.

"Okay," he snapped back. "Then you're sentencing her to die. Think about it. Right now, we can get to the mainland. Call for help," Young pleaded. "It's our only chance and we're likely not going to get another one. If you go back, you'll die and so will she."

A worm of indecision began to wriggle through his thoughts. What if Young was right? What if heading for the mainland was the only way to get help? But if Jett took Young away, what reason would there be for Ellsworth to keep Sarah alive? And if he took Young back, was he throwing away their only chance at escape? The seconds fizzed away like a fuse burning toward detonation.

His mind whirled until he settled upon the only solution he could think of, the only sure way toward rescue. He'd take the boat out into the channel, hail the nearest vessel and radio for help, then return to the island as quickly as he could. Sarah could stay hidden. The Channel Islands had nighttime fishing excursions, and the harbor patrol was on duty 24/7. Their office was located on the east side of the channel, and there was a coast guard station there, as well. They could contact someone quickly. Ellsworth might be filthy rich, but he wasn't going to beat the US Coast Guard.

Jett yanked the motor to life again and took the throttle. His gut was tight. If he was a praying man, he'd be pleading with God to keep Sarah safe until he got help. But his prayers had never made his father sober up, given his mother the strength to leave or restored Jett's health so he could resume his EOD duties. No answered prayers, just heartbreak, and he'd had enough of that. He was about to direct the craft toward the open sea.

"Jett." A voice came over the sound of churning water. "Listen to me." It was Tom, broadcasting over the radio from the docked vessel. "Turn the boat around right now and head back."

Yeah, right. Jett accelerated. *Because you're going to keep us safe and cozy in your nice island accommodations.*

"Return immediately, or we'll kill her."

His hand froze on the throttle, muscles taut as wire.

"They're bluffing," Young said. "Keep going. It's her only chance."

He was probably right. Tom hadn't left the dock, and the search was focused on finding Young. They would not have siphoned off the guards to hunt for Sarah. He throttled up until he heard what came next.

"Jett." It was Sarah's voice on the radio. The cold seeped in and around him. He blinked back a sudden blurring in his vision.

"Keep going," Young urged. "We've got to get away."

He listened, frozen.

"Jett, I'm here, with Tom," she continued, voice tinny over the radio. He almost didn't hear the last part over the crawling waves. "I'm sorry."

ELEVEN

Sarah was left in the charge of a man she'd heard Tom call Cy. The other man who'd caught her in the house had gone to assist Tom. She was shivering in the cold island air, something like a lump of ice settling in her stomach.

Cy hustled her out toward the dock, where Tom waited, hands on hips. Jett tied up the boat and climbed up to join them. With Cy covering both Sarah and Jett with his gun, Tom was free to retrieve Young.

He hauled him from the boat and shoved him against a piling with such force that Young cried out. Sarah could see blood trickling down Tom's shoulder from where Young's shot had grazed him, but he seemed oblivious.

Tom grabbed Young by the hair and ground his face to the rough wood. "Made a full recovery, huh? Well enough to steal a boat? You're not going to be well for long. You're gonna be dead, like you deserve."

The hatred that electrified his eyes froze Sarah in midstep. This was not a man simply acting on his boss's orders. Tom despised Del Young.

"What did he do to you?" Sarah said.

Tom didn't look at her.

"He did something to you, and you want revenge. What happened?"

He turned a deadly glare on her. "It's none of your business. Stay out of it." Tom grunted again in Young's ear. "No more stalling. It's time to meet with Mr. Ellsworth." He yanked Young away from the piling and frog-marched him back toward the golf cart. "Take them to the house and get him some dry clothes," Tom ordered his partner. "Mr. Ellsworth isn't going to want him dripping all over the rugs."

"We can't have damage to the Persian rugs, now can we?" Jett said, garnering himself a shove to the back from Cy that almost sent him to his knees.

Cy gestured for Sarah to fall in behind Jett, and he moved them toward the second parked cart. Jett's skin was prickled in goose bumps, water coursing off his sodden clothing. The water temperature couldn't be above sixty degrees, and there was a frigid wind blowing in on the front of what appeared to be a significant storm. Jett had to be freezing.

"I'm sorry," she said again as she came alongside. "The guard caught me in the downstairs hallway."

He shook his head. "Your ninja-detective skills need work, Sarah Gallagher."

She laughed. "I guess you're right."

They walked on in silence.

"What—" She pushed her wind-tossed hair behind her ears and found herself asking the question she could not get out of her mind. "I mean, what were you planning? I...it looked like you were setting a course toward open water."

He cocked his head, water snaking down from his temple to his strong chin. "I was figuring we would hail the nearest ship and then I'd return to get you."

She nodded. "That's what I thought," she said, hoping he did not hear relief in her voice.

"Sarah?" His eyes were riveted on hers now. "Did you think I was abandoning you?"

"No, of course not." Had she? Wasn't that exactly why her stomach had been in knots, though her mind knew better?

Tiny droplets of water spangled his thick lashes. She expected a joke or a cynical remark. Instead he sighed, a sound sadder than the low moan of the biting wind gusting up over the black rocks. "I wasn't the one who left, remember?"

She did. She would likely never forget the smallest detail of their anguished conversation right after he was suspended for fighting, halfway through their senior year. His behavior had become increasingly wild as his unemployed father's drinking and abuse escalated. And still, to the bitter end, he'd refused to talk to anyone about it, not her, not a counselor, not even Marco.

She knew Jett had wanted to leave town, but he'd feared what would happen to his mother. And, it grieved her to admit, he hadn't wanted to move away from her. She'd desperately wanted him to stay. Selfish, considering the price he'd had to pay. What did it cost a proud man like Jett to endure his father's abuse? To take beatings he knew would be visited on his mother otherwise?

Jett, I love you, I'll always love you, but I can't be with you anymore.

The guy threw the first punch, Sarah. What was I supposed to do? Walk away?

Yes, Jett. You were supposed to walk away, but you won't. And I can't stand to watch you self-destruct.

She remembered the way the light went out of his eyes then, like an extinguished candle. How could she let him go? But how could she not, when he was headed for catastrophe?

I thought love was supposed to be a forever thing, he'd said on that brilliant January morning.

She'd watched helplessly as he walked away, her heart cracking into a million tiny pieces. Why had she felt the same way watching him pilot the motorboat out of the cove? Surely she trusted him not to abandon her, even though there was no love between them. But since her father's death, she found it hard to trust her own emotions and decisions. "I didn't mean to imply that…" she called.

But he was not looking at her anymore, striding to the cart, tall and unyielding against the rain-washed night.

In that moment, she felt the heavy weight of defeat, and her heart cried out.

I'm tired of hurting, Lord. I'm tired of being scared. I'm sick of losing.

Recalling those long days in the hospital, she sometimes thought she could still smell the disinfectant, feel the stiff blankets around her legs. She recalled the favorite verse her mother read her every day during her extended hospital stay, over the beeping of the monitors, the endless prodding of the doctors.

These things I have spoken unto you, her mother had read, *that in me ye might have peace. In the world ye shall have tribulation: but be of good cheer; I have overcome the world.*

Tribulation? In the last forty-eight hours—indeed, the last several years—she'd had more than her fill of it. And oh, how much she'd lost—Jett, her father, her sense of safety, her confidence. She would let go her nursing profession, too, if she followed through on her plan to walk away from that. Was she a fool to think she should give that up to be a part of the family business? How much could she be expected to lose? Her father's weathered face surfaced in her memory, ever the tough marine with such tenderness for his wife and four girls that it took her breath away to recall it.

The grief swelled inside her and then a tiny trickle of comfort.

I've lost so much, but I haven't lost my God, she thought. And there was a sense of peace in that. She hurried to keep pace with Jett.

You've overcome the world, Father. Help me to overcome this.

Was she praying to Him about being imprisoned by a madman? Or the dark chasm that separated her from the man who had once been her everything? Perhaps she longed for God's power to overcome the thick blanket of grief that still lingered when she thought of her father or her own loss of confidence.

As they traveled back to the prison of Ellsworth's house, she was not sure.

Jett pulled on a pair of dry jeans tossed at him by Cy, over the monitoring bracelet around his ankle. The workman's shirt he put on next was heavy-duty and made for labor, which was fine by Jett. His nerves still tingled at how close he'd been to finding an escape route. Something else tugged at his insides as he pictured Sarah, standing in the veiled moonlight, eyes searching his face for signs that he'd betrayed her. He mulled it over as he waited for Cy to unlock the cell again.

She'd really thought he'd leave her? Was that truly what she believed him capable of, after all they'd shared? It was a knife to his heart. He recalled standing in the rain for three hours waiting for her to finish taking the SAT.

You waited? she'd said, her smile bright, cheeks pink.

'Course I waited, he'd replied with the proper dash of bravado. *Don't want my girl walking home alone.* It

was as though even now he could feel the imprint of her hand in his, the enormous joy at knowing Sarah Gallagher was his and no one else's.

That was years ago, Jett. You're both different people now. She doesn't know you, and you don't know her. Natural, he supposed, that after what she'd experienced she would be worried about him deserting her. Natural, but it stung anyway.

Or maybe, he thought with a surge of guilt, he'd walked away from her each time he'd messed up, lashed out. Maybe each of those outbursts were a method of pushing Sarah away until she had no choice but to cut him loose. Better for her to dump him, since he knew he could never willingly let her go. He'd known all along she was too good for him, and he'd gone out of his way to prove it. What was one more betrayal from him now? The twisting in his gut did not ease as he was escorted to the dining room.

Cy had already taken Sarah ahead to see to Young, he imagined. Young had better be a good talker, or they would all be killed in short order. Had he really forgotten where he'd stashed *The Red Lady* and Mary? Probably another lie. If Sarah would only take off her rose-colored glasses about the guy. But something in Young's words stuck with him when he spoke about Mary's love for him.

I didn't deserve it...

Quit going soft, Jett reprimanded himself. The guy had been ready to leave them behind and save his own skin.

They arrived at the same dining room where Jett had received his "gift" from Ellsworth. Sarah was sitting stiffly next to Ellsworth, who claimed the chair at the head of the table. Young sat in a chair away from the table, eyes on the carpet. His face was still marked with bruises, but his color was better, as if the near escape had jarred some life back into him. Tom stood behind him, anger puckering his brow.

Mr. Ellsworth was dressed in a pair of creased pants, a dark suit jacket and a button-up shirt. No tie. Maybe interrogation didn't require formal neckwear, Jett thought idly.

Jett was not offered a chair. He stood, legs splayed apart, pleased that at least they hadn't bound his hands again after his ill-fated escape plan. All eyes were on Ellsworth.

"How nice that you've regained your vigor, Mr. Young," Ellsworth said, fingers drumming on the table. "You always were the energetic type, weren't you?" Ellsworth glanced at Sarah. "Did you know he was hired to be my daughter's fencing coach? He came regularly to teach her, made himself at home enjoying all the diversions the island had to offer—that is, until he stole from me."

Ellsworth's expression was mild, but it was the kind of calm that settled over the water before a ferocious storm roared in.

Young didn't answer.

"Mr. Young taught fencing classes at the college, which is how he met my Mary at the end of her senior year. He suggested he give her private lessons." Ellsworth's mouth tightened. "He was using her, of course, to get close to my art collection."

Young's head snapped up. "You know how I felt about Mary."

"Oh, we do, don't we, Tom?"

Tom did not react except for a further souring of his expression.

"We know how you felt about Mary, and how she felt

about you after she realized you had stolen the Matisse from me."

"I gave it back."

"Yes, you did, didn't you, when Tom applied some persuasion." He gestured to Sarah again. "But he soon agreed to steal *The Red Lady* from Beretta for me to avoid prosecution."

"I tried to get it, but—"

Ellsworth held up a hand. "Yes, I know what you said. You were unable to complete the job. You promised to return my money. All lies. I should have dealt with you then, but Mary pleaded your case. For some reason, she was fond of you. Pity, I imagine she felt—it could be nothing else. All those Jet Ski excursions, the snorkeling adventures. It was sympathy, nothing more."

Jett wondered about that. Something was flowing underneath the conversation like a fast-moving current. What had happened on this island?

Ellsworth said, "You decided to strike off on your own, to keep my money and the painting and resell her to Beretta."

Young was still staring at the carpet.

Ellsworth got up and walked to Young, putting a hand on his shoulder, which made the man flinch. "That was your first mistake, thinking I would not find out that you really did steal her. Do you know what your second mistake was?"

Young chewed his lower lip.

"Abducting Mary," Ellsworth whispered.

Young's head shot up. "What?"

"Taking my daughter," Ellsworth said, louder.

"Can't you hear yourself? You're nuts." Young twisted to look at Tom and tried to rise. "You know he's nuts. Why are you going along with this?"

Tom slammed him back down in the chair. "Because you should be dead," he grunted. "You should have been the one."

The one?

"What are you talking about?" Sarah said, out of her chair now.

"He's crazy." Young's face was blotchy and pale. "I told you. He's insane. He's going to kill us all."

"I love my daughter," Ellsworth said.

"You don't love anything," Young shouted. "That's why you obsess about your art and your collections. You don't know how to feel, so you buy the work of painters and artists who did."

Ellsworth regarded him with cold silence.

"You don't love," Young said, voice dropping. "You possess. That's why you're alone."

"That's enough," Tom snapped.

"Perhaps he's right." Ellsworth scratched his chin thoughtfully. "I don't feel things properly. I never did experience emotions as strongly as others. I've never cared for anyone but my wife and daughter. Even when my wife was sick, I found I could not feel the way others would. Instead of pity or compassion, I felt almost a sense of anger at her for falling sick, and ultimately for leaving me." He looked to Sarah again. "Women feel everything so deeply—you can see their every thought and emotion as clear as paint on canvas. Like you, Ms. Gallagher."

Jett didn't like the way Ellsworth looked at her. He eased closer until he felt Cy's gun on his back, preventing him from moving any more.

"So perhaps it is true that I can only possess," he continued, now speaking to Young. "I strive to own and keep things." He paused. "But here's my little secret. Though I cannot feel, I like to be close to people who can feel everything—love, disappointment, joy…" He bent close to Young, whispering in his ear. "And pain." He smiled as he pulled a pen from his pocket and held it in front of Young's eyes. Jett's gut knotted. "Do you know what this is, Mr. Young? It's not just a writing implement, though it does write quite smoothly. Any guesses?"

Young stared blankly.

"No?" Ellsworth looked up. "Mr. Jett. I'm sure you're familiar."

Training to be an explosive ordnance disposal technician meant he'd done plenty of hours on combat skills and weaponry at the Naval Construction Battalion Center in Gulfport. He'd seen just about every kind of weapon imaginable, even this one. "It's a tactical pen." He didn't say the rest. Aircraft-grade aluminum with a carbide tip, capable of punching through flesh and breaking bones if used with enough force.

"Yes." Ellsworth gazed at the implement in his hand. "I've never hurt a man before, myself. But this time…" His gaze drifted to Young. "You're right. I don't feel many emotions, but I will be very close, so close, that I will experience every moment of your feelings, every second of your pain." A dreamy smile crossed his lips.

"No," Sarah said, moving toward Ellsworth until Tom barred her way. "He'll tell you. He'll tell you what you want to know. There's no reason to hurt him."

"There's a good reason, Sarah," Ellsworth said in a kindly voice. "I want to feel his pain." He held the pen in an ice-pick grip. Young tried to get out of the chair, but Tom held him in a fierce grip, eyes burning.

Sarah tried to step between them, but Jett grabbed her as Ellsworth raised the pen above his head, ready to slam it into Young's thigh.

"No," Young screamed, writhing in Tom's hold.

"Don't," Sarah cried out, trying to free herself from Jett.

Ellsworth's arm descended in a vicious arc.

Just as the lights were suddenly extinguished and the house plunged into darkness.

TWELVE

Sarah was immobilized by the darkness, but Jett was not. He grabbed her and pulled her to his side and toward the periphery of the room.

"Head for the door," he said, shoving her forward.

They had not gone five steps when Cy activated a flashlight and stuck his gun in Jett's face.

"Don't get any ideas."

"Lock them all up," Ellsworth was saying to Tom. "Check the electrical box. It's probably the storm."

"What if it's not?" Tom said, flicking on a Maglite he'd gotten from a pouch on his belt. "We talked about this possibility."

"It is the storm," Ellsworth snapped. "Now go see to it."

Tom led Young away, and Cy did the same with Sarah and Jett, escorting them back down to their cellar prison at a near jog. Sarah gasped as she stepped into her cell.

"There's water on the floor. The cellar must flood during a storm."

"That explains the water stains." Jett turned to Cy. "She needs to come in here with me. She'll get sick if she's wet and cold."

"She's got her own cell," Cy said.

A crackle came over his radio. "Get up here, now," Tom barked.

Sarah saw the hesitation on Cy's face. He wasn't the decision maker, and he didn't want to keep his boss waiting.

Jett had seen it there, too. "If she gets sick, there's no one here to help keep Young alive." He paused. "Or anyone else who gets hurt. You don't want that responsibility on your conscience, do you?"

Cy hesitated only a moment. Then he shoved both of them into Jett's cell and slammed and locked the door.

"Can we have a light, please?" Sarah asked. "It's pretty dark down here."

Cy pulled a penlight from his pocket and shoved it to Jett through the bars. Then he jogged out.

Sarah's feet were cold from the dousing. She tried to hug herself into some sense of warmth, but the chill of the temperature and the brutality she'd just witnessed remained. "What happened in that dining room? Ellsworth turned into a monster."

"He was already a monster." Jett grabbed the blanket from his cot and wrapped it around her, bundling her close to him. "Come here, you're cold."

Being in his arms again made her dizzy. She wished her senses would not respond so strongly to him, even after so many years had passed. "I'm okay."

"You're shivering."

She tried for a flippant remark to hide how very small she felt, how very safe in the circle of his embrace. "How come you're not cold? You were in the ocean trying to catch Young."

He ran his hands along her back and shoulders, chafing some warmth into them. "I'm navy. We don't get cold."

She sighed and leaned her head against him, giving in to the delicious warmth of his chest. She thought again of Ellsworth holding the pen, ready to slam it into Young's thigh, his face aglow with sick anticipation. "I didn't want to think that people could be like that, that they could brutalize each other for some piece of art to hang on a wall."

"You've never wanted to see the bad side in people," he said. "I guess it's all that church stuff."

She was too weary to engage him on this topic. "Why did the lights go out?"

His grip around her tightened a fraction. "Not sure."

"But you have an idea." His heart thudded a soothing rhythm against her cheek, and she wanted to rest in the steady beat, but his silence distracted her. She pulled back to study his face. It was impossible in the gloom.

He shrugged, making a show of tightening the blanket around her. "We're okay for now. That's the important point."

"Jett, I know you too well, so don't try to deceive me. What do you think is going on?"

"Probably just a short circuit. The storm and all that."

"Or?"

"Or nothing."

"I'm a detective, Jett, but even if I wasn't, I could tell that you're hiding something from me. I'm not going to let it drop, so you might as well say it. What else could have caused the blackout?"

He let out a breath. "The other party interested in Del Young."

"The other..." Her heart thunked against her ribs. "Antonio Beretta? Here on the island?"

"As I said, it's probably just the storm, but Beretta doesn't strike me as having a reputation for giving up."

She sank onto the cot, pulling her cold feet up underneath her. "Between Ellsworth and Beretta, I don't know who's crazier."

"My vote is Ellsworth. Beretta is a profit-driven drug lord, your typical ruthless thug, but Ellsworth has got something else going on altogether—something having to do with his daughter, I'd guess."

"Do you think Young is in love with Mary?"

"No idea. But it occurred to me that Mary might not have been abducted after all. Maybe she went willingly with Young. Ellsworth did say she was smart, and she must know on some level that her dad is a little short on sanity. Maybe she escaped with him under her own free will and Ellsworth can't admit that possibility."

"I had the same thought, but she's not making an effort to visit or contact her father."

"Would you?"

Would she? If her father was the manipulative and violent Ezra Ellsworth? "Could Mary possibly be involved in helping Young steal the painting from Beretta?"

"If she is," he said thoughtfully, "I hope she's got a real good hiding place."

She recalled the sickly eager look on Ellsworth's face as he held the tactical pen. *I want to feel his pain.*

Sarah squeezed her arms around herself to contain a shiver. "I have some good news."

"We could use it."

"Right before they caught me, I found the housekeeper's computer."

His eyes widened. "No joke?"

"No joke." It thrilled her to see the pride in his eyes. "I only had a second, but I sent an email to Candace. Only a few words. I told her we were alive but I didn't…"

She was interrupted as he took her hand, pulled her off

the cot, and swung her in a circle. "Now we're talking."
As he slid her to the floor, her mouth grazed his cheek.
Suddenly she wished she could feel one more of Jett's
kisses, the warm, emotion-filled contact she'd craved
when they were younger and the world was full of possibilities. If the past was truly past and they were free
to remember the reasons they'd loved each other instead
of the reasons they'd parted. His mouth moved closer to
hers as if he, too, craved the connection.

She angled her lips to his, body prickling with anticipation.

Then he set her on her feet and carefully moved back.

The message was clear. She'd made her choice, he was
reminding her, and he'd made his. The distance between
them could have been fathoms instead of feet. *Jett, what
happened to us?* she wanted to ask. Instead she made a
show of neatening her ponytail and looking through the
bars of the cell.

"I didn't have time to give her our location," she said.
"I told them I was alive, with you."

"They're detectives. They can find us, right?"

"They should be able to get a general vicinity by tracing the IP address."

He raised an eyebrow. "You have been studying, Detective Sarah."

She thought there might be a tone of respect under the
teasing, but she wasn't sure. Lifting a careless shoulder,
she pretended to search the space for any possible ways
out she hadn't noticed before.

"You really going to walk away from nursing and try
the PI gig?"

Was it mockery now in his tone? Or admiration? She
straightened. "Yes, if I have the courage." She wanted
to be brave, flippant, but instead the truth tumbled out.

"I… I have lost confidence in myself since, well, lately. I don't know why. It happened after the crash and the hospitalization and everything." She was dismayed to find that her voice caught on the last sentence.

He reached out to straighten the blanket that had slipped from her shoulders, and his hand lingered there, toying with her hair. "I understand. Better than you know."

She turned to him, hoping he would not see the moisture that had crept into her eyes. "What about you? Are you going to try to return to the navy in some other capacity?"

He sighed, the shutters falling into place, closing the momentary tenderness away. "No. I was medically discharged. Navy doesn't want damaged goods."

"You have a lot to offer the world, Jett, even if it isn't while wearing a uniform."

He stepped away, shaking his head. "This isn't where you are going to give me the 'God will use your circumstances for good' speech, is it?"

The cynical tone made her cringe. "No, but if I can start a new life, why can't you?"

"Because I haven't accepted the loss of my old one," he said. Before there would have been anger; now she heard only flat despair.

"It's really hard to make peace with something like that," she said softly.

"Yeah. It wasn't fair, and I didn't deserve to lose my career. I already got the raw deal with my father."

"That's the part you need to overcome, Jett. You're holding on to the terrible things that happened to you."

"And you aren't?"

"I'm trying really hard not to. I still struggle every day, and I ask Him to help me."

"I'm not going to ask God for anything, Sarah. He's not a fan of mine." His tone was brittle with loss, fraught with hurt and betrayal.

It pained her to know that part of that betrayal lay at her feet. "He doesn't want you to suffer. He wants to give you peace."

For a moment, his face took on a yearning expression. *He's the only one who can,* she wanted to whisper.

But he shook his head. "Save it for someone else, Sarah. I don't need you to minister to me. I'm fine."

The connection between them was severed. The cold seemed to intensify, and the darkness grew even more impenetrable. Hurt throbbed inside her. *What did you expect? That the current situation would suddenly make him see the truth?* He thought she was a naive, misguided do-gooder, blindly following a God who didn't care. That hadn't changed at all.

A muted bang on the ceiling and the sound of running feet drew their attention. "Keep on your toes, and if you can get away, run and hide for as long as you can."

"What's going on?" Sarah murmured, more to herself than him.

"We're about to find out," he said, pushing her behind him as the cellar door was flung open.

Jett's muscles bunched, tension coiling through him at being caged like sitting ducks for whoever was jogging—no, sprinting—through the cellar toward them. He went to the bars, offering himself as a nice big target in case anyone was looking for one. Maybe they would see Sarah's cell door open and figure she was somewhere else on the property. The darkness was their only advantage at the moment, and it was a pretty minute one.

Tom emerged, flashlight in hand. He was moving fast, face grave, breathing hard.

"What's going on?"

"Beretta's men are here."

Jett's heart sank at the confirmation. Why couldn't he have been wrong about that? Beretta was not a man to be thwarted any more than Ellsworth. He and Sarah were caught between two lunatics.

"They cut the power," Tom said. "They're going to make a run on the house. We're barricaded in, but we can't hold for long with the weaponry they've got. Three men is our initial count. Arrived in a fast boat and took out our guy at the docks and one on the property."

He unlocked the door and opened it. The hinges swiveled with a squeal of protest. "Cy is taking Ellsworth and Young to the helicopter. There's not room for everyone."

"So what's going to happen to us?" Sarah said.

His mouth tightened. "If Beretta's men find you, they'll torture you for information on Young and then kill you when they've heard enough."

Sarah shook her head in disgust. "Torture and violence. And you call yourself men."

Jett didn't doubt it about the torture, but Beretta's methods would be simpler, more brutal—a baseball bat or a bullet instead of a tactical pen. His ribs were still sore from the beating he'd gotten in Playa del Oro. "Torture seems to be the standard operating practice around here."

Tom hustled them away from the cage and toward towering wooden racks that extended into the darkness with an eighteen-inch gap between them. He stopped and gestured them forward to the narrow space between the two.

"If you go sideways, you can fit. There's a door about a hundred yards down. You can get out of the mansion. Hide until it's over."

"Now you're letting us go? I didn't know you cared."

"I don't. I'm protecting Mr. Ellsworth's assets. That's what I'm paid to do."

"It's not just about the money," Sarah said. "Is it? What did you mean when you said Del Young should have been the one?"

"No time. Get moving," he commanded.

Jett dug in his heels. "Take off my tracking bracelet. Beretta's men can use it to find me."

"We've disabled the program on the house computers." Tom tapped his pocket. "But I can still find you on my mobile phone. Don't think we're through with you. This isn't over until Mr. Ellsworth has *The Red Lady* back."

"And Mary," Sarah put in.

A strange look crossed his face. "Yeah. Go now. This is going to be a battle, and the outcome should be decided in a couple of hours. Lie low until then."

Jett stared at him incredulously. "Where, exactly, are we supposed to go? This island can't be more than twenty kilometers from bow to stern. Where do you suggest we hide from a team of murderous thugs?"

Tom's smile was cruel. "You're navy right? What's your motto—*Semper Fortis*? Always strong? You'll think of something."

Jett thought about the EODs' unofficial motto, Initial Success or Total Failure. He'd always been willing to put his own life on the line, but now there was Sarah to think about. But what was the other choice? To leave her here with Tom, who would likely be overpowered and killed by Beretta's men anyway? *Rock and a hard place, Jett, just like always.*

"Call in the police," Sarah said. "You know there's no way you can survive this."

"I know the island, and we have a few protections in

place. I can win." He pushed them forward. "Go, before
I change my mind and leave you caged here for Beretta
to find."

Jett's mind whirled with possibilities. They had to get
to a boat. Immediately.

Initial Success or Total Failure.

He looked at Sarah, who was already shivering in
the cold but still standing straight, chin up. Though he
could not see it, he hoped there would be that gleam in
the green gold of her eyes, that light that meant she would
go down swinging. He recalled the time he'd crashed his
motorcycle after taking a stupid dare and woken up in the
hospital to find her there standing next to his mother. His
mom was hysterical, frayed edges showing in the tightly
clasped fingers and trembling shoulders. Sarah was praying with her, whispering a plea for healing and God's
presence to invade the room. He didn't know what he'd
felt when he heard that, a rush of something that might
have been a profound sense of peace. More likely it was
just relief that his father was not there and pleasure at
finding the woman who was his heartbeat standing there
praying for him as if he were the most important man
in the world. Dominic Jett, worthy of prayer, worthy of
love. How could she believe that? About him?

A cold draft whispered along through the passage
down which Sarah had already started. She stopped,
turned to him and reached out her hand.

"Jett?"

He imagined the unspoken questions. *Are we delivering ourselves up to Beretta's men? Will we ever escape
this island? Are we going to die here?*

The cold washed over him, at odds with the burning
that ribboned through his body. He knew he would do
anything, sacrifice anything to get her back home safely

to her family. She wasn't his anymore, but he would still die for her if that's what it came down to. He wasn't worthy of prayer, worthy of love, but maybe that was the only way he had left to care for Sarah Gallagher.

A tremor went through him. What if he couldn't complete this impossible mission? Like he'd failed at keeping his mom from being beaten? The way he'd lost the career that was more important to him than breathing?

You lost, time and time again. You lost.

Sarah's words came back to him. *That's the part you need to overcome, Jett. You're holding on to the terrible things that happened to you... He wants to give you peace.*

I don't need peace, he thought bitterly. *I need to win. Just this once.* His resolve hardened into granite. With Sarah depending on him, he would overcome. Right here, right now, with only his muscles and his brains to rely on, and God could have a front-row seat.

"All right," he said, "let's do this."

THIRTEEN

Sarah struggled against the sense of unreality as they squeezed through the wooden racks, the moist wood clammy where it brushed her shoulders. Here they were, on the run again, trying to escape like it was some sort of bad movie. At least in a movie, the script was already written. The outcome was far from decided for Sarah and Jett. Things were going from bad to horrendous.

"God, please help us," was all she could manage as they shuffled along. She hoped He would hear the rest, a plea for safety for them both and for Del Young. Her senses were slow, dulled with the same thick, stupefying fear that she'd felt when her car plunged over the cliff.

The silent scream from that awful day still rang in her memory. She remembered him holding onto the door handle with one hand, the other reaching out to her as if he was trying to protect her, even in the very last moments of his life. Her dad, her hero, gone in a moment.

It could end the same now, her nerves whispered. *You could die, you and Jett, just like Dad.* The fear twisted tighter around her until she was almost paralyzed with it. It was so cold, so dark, the evil pressing in on all sides.

Jett seemed to sense something was wrong. He held his hand out and took hers and pressed her knuckles to his mouth for a soft kiss. No words passed between them, but his touch, the warmth of his kiss, gave her just enough strength to keep going, one stumbling foot sliding next to the other.

In moments, they'd reached a metal door, unlocked it and pushed through. Cold air doused her face and confused her senses after her stint in the cage. She held up an arm against the falling drops that pelted her head. They were at the edge of the back lawn of the estate, rain pattering against the neatly trimmed grass. It was a wide hedged-in area, complete with gravel paths and an ostentatious fountain gurgling away in the middle. Looking up she could see the ledge where Young had jumped rather than endure a confrontation with Ellsworth. Now she understood why.

She followed Jett's lead and flattened herself against the wall of the house, staying away from the glow cast by the landscape lighting. A shout came from somewhere close by.

Jett pointed to a dense patch of shrubbery at the far side of the lawn. "We'll go there," he whispered, lips against her temple. "Ready to run?"

She nodded, prickles teasing her skin. He counted to three, and they sprinted across the turf. From the front of the house came the sound of splintering glass. They increased their speed until she could hardly keep from slipping on the wet grass. Would they be shot in their escape? The skin on the back of her neck crawled, and she felt completely exposed, utterly vulnerable, like a rabbit running across an open field, avoiding the falcon.

Making it to the far hedge, they squeezed through a gap in the bushes. Panting, they stopped to listen for sounds of pursuit. There was nothing but the wind blowing through the branches of the scrubby pines.

"Let's head for the dock," Jett murmured. "We can take the motorboat and go for help."

She hesitated, thinking of Del Young, but he was being bundled off by helicopter, so there was nothing she could do for him now. They hurried down the slope, keeping off the road and under the minimal cover provided by a scattering of oak and pine.

The island appeared to be carved from one massive black stone tossed up from the ocean. The only flat part, it seemed to Sarah, was the location of Ellsworth's mansion. Loose rock shifted under their feet, forcing them to slow. A piece broke away and rolled down past her, picking up speed as it went. Her calves complained about the effort, and she suddenly felt the accumulated scrapes and bruises that covered her body.

"We're coming up on the peak where we can look down into the cove."

"Would Beretta's men leave the boats unguarded?" she panted.

"I'm hoping they think everyone left is defending the house now that Ellsworth is taking the chopper."

She scanned the dark sky. The moon was veiled in wispy clouds, not a star showing. "I haven't seen it leave yet."

"It hasn't." He pointed to a flat cutout on a projection of rock that looked out over the waves. The chopper was barely visible on the landing pad.

"It must be taking them a while to secure Young and move him there."

Or Beretta's men caught them already, she thought. No doubt the idea had occurred to Jett, as well. She worried her lip between her teeth.

"They left us to fend for ourselves, Sarah," he said. "Don't waste too much pity on them."

"Young is a pawn in all this."

"He messed up his life. Now he's messing up ours. I got no sympathy."

The steel was back in his eyes, his voice, so unforgiving it made her want to draw back. "Where's your tender side, Jett?"

"I was never tender."

"I beg to differ. A guy who brought Mrs. Grossman's old retriever a twenty-pound sack of kibble each month?"

He arched an eyebrow. "I didn't know you knew that."

"Mrs. Grossman can't keep a secret."

He shrugged. "It was no big deal. She couldn't drive, and the bags were too heavy. That was an exception."

"Jett—" she traced the wet hair stuck onto his forehead "—you can't fool me. I know you."

"You knew me when I thought I could make things turn out all right." His hand hovered over hers, trailing over the back of her hand until a new set of prickles danced across her skin. "I'm not that dumb kid anymore."

"Maybe you're turning into the man God wants you to be."

For an instant his face was gentle as he considered. "But I've lost everything. If He cared about me at all, why would He want me to fail?"

She weighed her words carefully, sensing the moment was precious. "Because God does His best work with failures."

Was there a moment when he turned over the thought in his mind? A brief lowering of the barrier he'd put up between him and God? The seconds lingered, cradled by the wind and waves until they blew away into the night.

Jett shook his head and turned. "We've got to keep going."

The way became steep for several hundred yards. Jett

took her hand and helped haul her up until they crested the high point of the cliff. Crouching made her sodden clothes cling to her like a second skin as she panted, gazing down into the harbor.

Jett peered into the darkness. "The motorboat is still there, and the forty footer. No sign of Beretta's vessel, so they must have secured it elsewhere."

He started to speak, and she put a finger across his lips. "Don't even tell me to stay here while you check it out. Come on."

"You…"

She pressed her finger to keep his mouth closed. "Time is money, navy man. Let's go."

She moved by him, ignoring her squelching shoes, which did nothing for her dignity. He mumbled something and started after her. They ran along the plunging slope toward the dock, stopping to listen every few paces. The motorboat was sitting as it had been, shifting silently in the waves. The quiet made her skin crawl. Beretta's men were there, somewhere, waiting in the darkness.

Shoving down the fear, she ran after Jett to the motorboat and climbed aboard.

Her heart slammed against her ribs. So close to escape. So close. She strained her ears for any sound of the helicopter, but there was still nothing but the sound of the sea.

Thrilled as she was at their possible escape, she wondered what Del Young's fate would be if he truly could not remember where *The Red Lady* and Mary were holed up.

Jett put his hand on the throttle. "Hope the rain will mask the sound."

In the distance they heard a loud crack. Thunder? Or a gunshot? Jett hurried to loose the lines from the cleats.

Sarah moved to the stern, set the engine to start and

tugged the starter cord. The engine warbled to life with a sound that was more beautiful to her ears than a symphony. Freedom. It was so close she could taste it. The channel glittered, distant and serene, waiting to receive them.

The engine powered up and chugged the little boat along.

No sign of pursuit. They were going to make it. She almost laughed out loud in her relief.

As they moved away from the dock, the sound of helicopter blades broke the silence.

The chopper flew into view, low over the water, sending salty spray into the air. Inside the craft, he thought she made out Ellsworth's silver hair in the rear. Though Young was not safe with Ellsworth, at least he too had escaped Beretta's clutches.

Jett steered toward the ocean, and with every foot between them and the dock, Sarah's spirits rose. She felt like shouting with joy. The ordeal was over. Beretta's men would not dare take action once they cleared the harbor. Though five of the islands were uninhabited national park land, they would be plenty visible in the Santa Barbara Channel. Beretta would not linger there. At least, she did not think he would. He was ruthless, but she did not think he was stupid.

The helicopter was almost over them now, the rotor action whipping the spray into her eyes, blinding her. So they would make an escape, too. Would Ellsworth elude punishment for abducting three people? Marco and her sisters would use the full resources of the agency to help the police bring him to justice. For now, that would have to do. Her thoughts were cut short when a series of holes suddenly appeared in the windshield of the chopper. At first she could not understand what had happened.

She didn't hear the shots, but suddenly another string of bullets peppered holes into the metal front and sides of the chopper.

"Jett," she screamed.

"Get down." He pulled her to her knees to the bottom of the boat.

In shock, she watched the helicopter plunge toward them.

Jett jerked the motorboat throttle hard to port and the vessel responded. He dared not risk a look behind at the chopper as it dropped out of the sky, deadly rotors slicing the air with the force of a stun grenade. The cove echoed with the shriek of the chopper's protesting engine, and wind from the churning blades buffeted the waves.

The thing was falling right on top of them.

One blade smashed down inches from the gunwale. Sarah screamed. He wanted to yell for her to hunker down in the bottom of the boat, but he was struggling with the movement, willing the motorboat to outrun the helicopter blades that would surely cut them to ribbons or crush them to death.

Another blade ripped into the stern, inches from where he was standing. The metal on metal sounded like a human cry as sparks flew from the impact. An airborne piece of hot metal burned through his shirt and onto his bicep, but he did not let go of the throttle. The boat bucked and swayed due to the whirling crash currents, taking on water. Pieces of shattered glass thundered down into the bottom of the motorboat. Sarah pitched forward, clinging to the side.

"Faster," she screamed.

Another hunk of metal spiraled through the air before it splashed into the ocean, blinding him with spray. He pushed the boat as fast as the engine could handle.

Inch by inch he pulled away from the epicenter of the wreck. One yard, then two. Sweating and breathing hard, he finally risked a look back.

The chopper was on its side in about fifteen feet of water, what was left of the blades still straining to do their job as the craft began to settle to the bottom. The bullets had punched through the front window and probably killed the pilot. Water sucked in through the splintered glass, speeding the chopper on its way to the bottom of the cove. The fate of those in the backseat was uncertain, but he saw no signs of movement.

Uneasily he scanned the cliff tops. In the dark, it was impossible to tell where the shooter was holed up, nor did he want to take the time to find out.

He pulled her to the stern. "Keep going toward the channel. Get help from whoever you can."

She opened her mouth to answer, but he was already climbing onto the gunwale, preparing to dive.

Her eyes were wide, lashes flecked with water. They shone, marvelous in the moonlight and for a moment he wished he could stop everything and just soak in the sight of her.

"You're going to try and get them out?" she said, mouth agape.

"Yeah. Not that they deserve it."

Her lips quirked into a smile. "I thought Mrs. Grossman was the exception."

He rubbed a hand across his face. "I did, too. Keep your head down."

"Jett—" she started.

"Yeah?"

"I'll pull the boat up as close as I can to help with the victims."

"No," he snapped as firmly as he could manage. "The shooters are coming back. Get out. Get help. Please."

Her expression didn't change. It was serene somehow, and suffused with something. Could it be pride in him? No, he didn't think so, but it was a delicious notion for the second he entertained it.

"Jett," she said, "we're going to do this together."

"No, we're not." Was he really having this argument with a helicopter wreck in the background and armed shooters combing the island?

She just smiled at him. "Normal women would head for the channel, you know," he snapped, realizing he was once again going to lose.

"Who said I was a normal woman?"

He could think of nothing to reply to that.

"Dive, Mr. Navy Man," she said sweetly. "They're running out of air."

Marco often said the Gallagher sisters would have made great combat soldiers. Jett figured Marco was wrong on that count. If Sarah was representative of the whole clan, they'd be discharged for disobeying orders in a flash. He dived, grumbling to himself all the way down. He imagined Sarah laughing at him from the surface.

FOURTEEN

Fortunately, the lights from the helicopter were still operating and the soft glow showed Jett the way through the turbulence. He kicked hard through the swirling water and made it to the cockpit, peering through the ruined glass. There was no sign of the pilot. He'd probably not had time in the course of their hurried departure to fasten himself in and the impact of the crash had ejected his body into the ocean. Unlikely he'd filed a flight plan. Poor guy. Jett hoped it had been quick and painless.

Jett figured since the chopper hadn't even cleared the cliffs before it was shot down, there would likely be no attention from the coast guard or the harbor patrol, either. They were on their own, like they had been since the start of this whole surreal situation.

He swam to the body of the aircraft, tugging on the door. It would not budge due to the pressure of the water. Leveraging himself on a landing skid, he tried to heave the door open. Through the glass, he could make out Ellsworth and Young. Ellsworth sat in his chair, looking calm and composed as the water began to fill the interior, as if he was waiting for instructions. Young lolled in his seat, eyes closed and his head slumped forward onto his chest.

Jett's lungs were burning. It was nothing near the excruciating dive training he'd received in EOD school. At least no one was whacking at him the way his instructors used to do to gauge his level of calm in the water. He returned to the cockpit window and started to kick out the shattered glass. He'd made a sizable hole when his ears started to ring and his vision blurred.

Not now, he hissed, but the fuzziness remained, and he knew he didn't have much time.

He used to be able to hold his breath underwater for more than three minutes. Thanks to his head injury, he'd lost his edge, along with his dignity and more of his confidence than he'd like to admit. Maybe he was weakened due to exhaustion.

He thought about Marco's favorite saying—*I don't stop when I'm tired. I stop when I'm done.*

The memory fueled his strength, and he kicked out again, widening the hole until the dizziness almost overwhelmed him. Frustration churning in his gut, he kicked up to the surface, sucking in a breath, hoping his vision would clear.

Sarah spotted him immediately.

"What's the status?" she called.

After a moment to suck in some oxygen, he gasped out what he knew, using the time to try to get his system back online. The dizziness was subsiding, and he thought his vision was clearing.

"I'm gonna go back down in a sec…" His words trailed off when she jumped into the water with him.

"What are you doing?"

"I anchored the boat." She shook the hair out of her eyes, splattering him in the process. "I'm helping you since you can't bring them both up at once."

"No way, Sarah. You are not going down there."

She smiled, face unbearably lovely and mischievous

in the sliver of moonlight. "Haven't we established by now that you aren't the boss of me?" She left him there, mouth open, and kicked away down into the water.

Pulling in another deep breath and hoping his body would cooperate, he trailed her down.

The rest of the cockpit window came away easily, and they swam past the pilot's seat and surfaced in the cabin air pocket. The water level had risen. It was nearly to the unconscious Young's head, a precious eighteen inches of oxygen keeping them from drowning. Ellsworth was standing on his seat now, head close to the ceiling, eyeing them.

"What's happened?" he demanded.

"Beretta's men shot you down," Jett explained. "Your pilot is dead."

"How do I get out of here?"

Obviously he wasn't going to lose any sleep over his pilot's death. "You're going to swim out the cockpit window and up to the surface. We've got the boat ready."

"I don't know how to swim."

Jett sighed. A guy who owned his own island didn't take the time to learn to swim? "Then I'll tow you."

Ellsworth cocked his head again in that birdlike manner, wary. "And why would you do that?"

He didn't know how to answer for a moment. "Something to do with an old lady and dog kibble," he said finally. He turned to Sarah, who was checking Young for a pulse.

"He's alive." She unfastened his harness and crooked her arm around his neck. "I'll cover his nose and mouth and get to the surface as fast as I can."

He debated. Was it better for him to accompany Ellsworth, who might panic and fight, or Young, who was a dead weight? At the rate the cabin was filling, he didn't have time to get Ellsworth to the boat and return for Young. It would have to work.

He gave Sarah a stern look. "All right, but if it becomes too much, get yourself to the surface and leave Young to me."

She nodded.

"Okay," he said to Ellsworth. "You're going to take a deep breath and hold it. You can grab onto my shirt and I'll guide you."

He could see the muscles knotting in Ellsworth's throat. "I do not think I can do that."

Jett's patience was ebbing low. "If you want to live, you don't have a choice."

Sarah was already swimming past him, towing the inert Del Young along. He gave her a nod with more assurance than he felt. "I'll be right behind you."

"You'd better be," she said, in a tone that reminded him of Marco. She took a breath and disappeared with her patient under the water.

He turned back to Ellsworth. The water had risen another few inches, and his head was jammed against the metal side in the precious pocket of air. His mouth was pinched, the skin of his face an unnatural pallor, as if he was carved from a piece of white stone.

"I…" He swallowed convulsively. "There is something wrong. With my body."

Jett looked for signs of outward trauma, but he saw none. Didn't matter anyway. The top of the triage list was to prevent the guy from drowning—everything else would have to wait.

"We'll check you over after we get out of here."

Ellsworth wasn't listening. "My heart is pounding and there is a tension in my stomach. I feel light-headed."

Jett looked on incredulously as the water crept up his chin. "Mr. Ellsworth, that's called fear."

"Fear." Ellsworth cocked his head.

"Yes, fear. You must have felt it before."

"Only once, three months ago," he said faintly. "But I did not know it was fear."

The guy was certifiable.

"What should I do?" He turned gray eyes on Jett, searching for some answer to a problem that was way beyond Jett's ability to fix.

What did a person do with fear? What did Jett do with his?

"You beat it down," Jett said. "You're gonna shove it back, hold your breath, and I'm going to get you out of here."

Ellsworth seemed to be considering Jett's words, but there was no more time for talk since there were only six inches of air remaining.

He took Ellsworth's arm. "Deep breath and here we go." With a hard tug, he forced Ellsworth off the chair and into the water. The man's hands clamped around Jett's arm. He propelled them to the cockpit and out the shattered window.

The going was slow after that. Ellsworth did not have the instinct to help kick, and he was a dead weight. Jett finally maneuvered himself behind Ellsworth and grabbed him around the neck, swimming on his back as hard as he could. Lights sparked in his field of vision. Ellsworth's fingers clawed into his arms and the distance to the surface seemed interminable. The ringing started up in his head now, louder, overwhelming his senses. He felt his muscles numbing, as if they were slowly icing over, his limbs growing heavy.

You can do this, Jett, he told himself. *Mental toughness. Don't stop until you're done.*

He kicked with all his might. There were no more than eight feet left to the surface, but he began to lose ground, drifting back, victim of an irreversible pull that was sucking him down toward the wreck, toward his death.

"No," he cried out in his mind. Desperately he tried to kick harder, to pull through the water with his free arm. His chest burned and his limbs moved in slow motion. He would succeed; he would overcome this small distance between life and death.

But his body began to close in on itself, his vision narrowing down into two tiny pinpricks and then blinking off into darkness.

Sarah pulled and shoved Del Young into the motorboat. She sat on her knees, panting, muscles trembling from the effort. Forcing herself into motion, she checked her victim's vitals. He was breathing. Her spirits lifted until she felt his pulse die away under her fingers.

Lacing her palms together, she began compressions, fighting against her shivering to keep a steady rhythm.

"Come on, Mr. Young," she hissed. "Don't quit on me now."

All the while she was performing the compressions she kept glancing toward the water, waiting to see Jett and Ellsworth make it to the surface.

After a full cycle she checked Young's pulse. There it was, the tiny flutter of motion that marked the presence of the most divine gift. His heart continued to beat, and he breathed in shallow gusts.

She rolled him on his side, wishing she had a blanket to put over him. Peering over the bow, she scanned for the shadows of Jett and Ellsworth, but she saw nothing.

How long had it been? She'd lost track of time in the arduous journey with Young in tow and the seemingly endless CPR. She leaned over the side of the bobbing motorboat, staring until her eyes burned. Surely they should have resurfaced by now. A moment more, she'd give them a moment more.

The seconds ticked away and still no sign of them. Bubbles rose to the surface as the helicopter settled deeper into ruin. Had Jett turned back for some reason? Or Ellsworth panicked and fought him?

She was scrambling over the side to dive in again when a figure rose, thrashing and gulping air.

"Help me," Ellsworth said, voice high with panic.

She grabbed his clothes and pulled. He surged over the side and into the bottom of the boat, water streaming off his suit jacket. Gasping, he got to his knees, hands braced against the bottom.

"Where's Jett?"

He didn't answer, wiping at the rivulets pouring from his hair.

"Where's Jett?" she snapped, gripping his arm and forcing him to look at her.

"I don't know." He peered around him. "We need to get back to land."

"We've got to get Jett."

Ellsworth blinked at her. "If he isn't here by now, he's probably drowned. There's no sense looking for him." He scanned the boat as if he was trying to figure out how to raise the anchor.

"But he rescued you," she said, staring in utter disbelief. "And you'd leave him to die?"

Ellsworth turned a distracted gaze on her. "Who?" he said.

Who? Ellsworth stared at her with the bland, innocent expression of a child. How had his heart become so warped that he could feel no compassion, no concern even for the man who'd risked his life to save him?

"Mr. Ellsworth," she said, "while you're down on your knees, why don't you pray to God to restore your soul?"

An odd expression crossed his face. "You are so like my Mary," he said. "So very much like her."

Unable to look at him one more moment, she scoured the water, praying, pleading with God that she would see a dark head surfacing, that roguish smile chiding her for her worry, ribbing her for doubting, mocking her for praying.

The seconds ticked by in slow motion.

No Jett.

"We need to go," Ellsworth said, gripping her wrist.

She wrenched free. "I'm not leaving him."

"I have to contact Tom. It is very urgent."

She turned away, no longer listening.

"Would you risk your life for someone who is probably already dead?" he said.

For Jett? She already knew the answer. Her mind filled with a tidal wave of fear, she dived over the side.

FIFTEEN

Jett felt his consciousness slipping away, and he was powerless to stop it. He sank slowly toward the wreck, vision blurred, his ears roaring. His muscles, bones and other systems had shut off, as if a plug had been pulled. He knew he should feel cold, scared, but he was numb in both mind and body. Was he in the water or floating through space? Try as he might, his senses would not come back online.

So it was going to come to this. The thought floated up from some corner of his brain that was still functioning. It would be the ocean that took his life, the sea that he'd loved since he was old enough to walk. The mad, crashing waves had always meant freedom, an escape from the disappointments found on terra firma, the people there that had let him down.

He'd thought maybe it would be an IED that got him one day, as he went about his navy duties. Or perhaps a motorcycle wreck—one minute he'd be jazzed about the speed, pumped by adrenaline as he drove along the incomparable California coast, and the next he'd be gone. And that would be that. The end. Mission over.

All the struggle, the anguish he'd known at the hands of a father who was supposed to nurture him, a mother whose job it was to protect him, twirled through his consciousness in a trail of thudding misery. Why had everything gone wrong? What was it about Dominic Jett that invited punishment instead of love? The little boy heart inside him cried out to his father. *Why didn't you love me more than the alcohol? Wasn't I worth it?*

He thought of Sarah, the woman who had rejected him because he had not been able to bury his anguish deep enough. Did she wonder if she wasn't worth it? Had Sarah believed he could have changed his own self-destructive ways if only she'd been important enough to him? Worthy enough? *I'm sorry, Sarah.* He brimmed with grief that she would never hear him utter the words. Had his own father said he was sorry, in some silent moment as he watched his boy cry? Did he ever wish things had been different? Craved a life that was not dispensed by the bottle? Now as he floated helplessly, there was no anger left, only puzzlement. So many walls he had been unable to climb in his twenty-six years, unable to overcome with determination and grit. What had it meant, his life? A failed career, a messed-up family, a body that was about to let him down one last time. And then nothing.

How long would it take him to drown? Already he knew he would have to inhale soon, to let in the vast ocean that pressed at his closed mouth.

He thought about a verse Sarah had read aloud to him after he'd been suspended from high school the first time for drinking.

These things I have spoken unto you, that in me ye might have peace. In the world ye shall have tribulation: but be of good cheer; I have overcome the world.

He'd tried all his life to be an overcomer, but now the word that resonated in his soul was *peace*. The idea twirled through his mind like a warm sunbeam, piercing the cold that pressed in on every side. How tantalizing to imagine his spirit floating in a state of peace instead of despair.

I have overcome the world.

The world, and everything in it, his soul whispered to him. Every sin, every disappointment, each failing, every pain. To overcome it all would take a very big God, the kind that Sarah served.

...in me ye might have peace.

Peace. How he craved it then, more than he'd ever desired anything. More than love, more than forgiveness, more than victory.

"God," he said as the darkness started to close in. "I want Your peace."

And then he closed his eyes.

Sarah ignored the terror that enveloped her as she saw Jett floating below the waves with his arms flung wide, his body moving at the mercy of the tide. She clamped her arms around him and kicked for the surface.

Oh, God, please, she silently screamed. She prayed with everything in her in that endless journey to the surface. They broke the waterline, and she heaved in a breath, desperately hoping that Jett's body would respond to the sweet gift of air and do the same. Instead, he was limp and still.

"Jett," she yelled in his face, fingers scrambling for a pulse in his neck. Was there a heartbeat? Movement? Her fingers were shaking so bad she couldn't tell, her cheek so cold she could not feel his breath on her face.

"Help me," she screamed to Ellsworth, spinning around to locate the motorboat.

Only it wasn't there. The vessel was making steady progress toward the channel with Ellsworth at the throttle.

It took her a moment for reality to penetrate her shock. He'd left them. After Jett had saved his life. He had pulled up the anchor and abandoned them.

Anger burned hot and bright inside her as she grabbed Jett and shook him hard.

"Dominic Anthony Jett, you wake up right this minute, do you hear me?"

His head fell sideways. She shook him again, harder. "You don't want me to tell Marco that you went and died on me, do you? He'll have your ears. He'll say you were a quitter. Is that what you are, Jett?"

Tears started down her face as she desperately tried to rouse him. He didn't stir and she looked frantically around for someone, for any kind of help. There was nothing but dark waves and the hiss of the helicopter wreckage disappearing under the rising water. She'd never felt so completely alone in her life. Terror stripped away at her courage until she could barely move for the heavy weight of fear.

"Come on, Sarah. Do something."

She had to get to land so she could attempt CPR. She crooked her arm under his chin and began straining toward shore against the waves that seemed determined to yank them out to open water. She made only a few feet of progress before she had to stop and rest.

"Jett," she yelled again, hardly able to breathe through the unshed tears clogging her throat. "Jett, don't leave me." She could not even feel the tears that blurred her vision and spilled down her face. Again, she tried to swim for shore, and again, she did not have the strength to fight the waves.

She cradled him to her, wrapping her arms around his back and pressing her face to his, treading water to keep them both barely afloat. Stroking his wet face, she gave in to the anguish. Her lips to his mouth, she kissed him, crying, speaking meaningless words of grief. She had never stopped thinking about him, that broken teen, that scarred adult, and now he was lost to her forever.

No. She would not allow her fears to become fact.

When she felt them drifting farther away from shore, she tried again, towing Jett along until every muscle in her body screamed its displeasure, kicking at the water with furious chops, her arms clawing ahead, fighting against a vast enemy of sucking salt water.

A desperate animal cry escaped her lips as her efforts were rendered useless. The shore remained as far away as ever, and Jett was still and silent as the grave. There was only dark and cold and the endless rasping waves.

The clouded sky offered no comfort as she tried again to rest and reconnoiter. It was a massive effort to both tread water and hold Jett steady, to keep him from being pulled from her grip and whirled away. Her fingers were knotted, cramped and painful. The water temperature was slowly rendering her numb.

She tried one last time to make headway against the violent surge.

"God help me," she tried to yell, but it came out no louder than a broken whisper.

Something shifted, and suddenly her movement became easier. For one terrified moment she thought she had lost her grip on Jett and he'd floated free of her grasp, but when she turned, she encountered his dark eyes, open and alert, his arms paddling weakly in the water in an effort to help them move.

"Jett!" she screamed, swallowing a mouthful of water that left her coughing.

He gave her a wan smile. "Hey, Sarah Gal. Don't drink the salt water."

"I thought…I…I…" And then she began to cry for all she was worth until he wrapped her in an embrace. She was dreaming—she'd wanted him to wake up so badly that her senses were lying to her, cruelly tricking her. But his arms were there, she could feel them, keeping her close, anchoring her to him against the waters that would tear them apart.

"Are you real?" she whispered, her fingers seeking his cold face.

He gave her a tender smile and kissed her forehead. "Yes, ma'am, as far as I can tell."

When she got control of her shuddering body, she looked again at him, putting her hands on his temples, stroking her fingers over his cheeks and chin to reassure herself that he was really alive. He let her explore, treading water to keep them afloat.

There was an unidentifiable expression on his face, but she could not make out quite what in the darkness. "You wouldn't wake up," she sniffed, voice breaking again.

"Better late than never." His voice was weak. "I thought I was a goner, but then my eyes opened up again. God's not done with me, I guess."

She laughed, which sounded slightly hysterical to her own ears. "Ellsworth took the boat. He knew you were down there and he just left. Can you believe that?"

"Sadly, yes."

"We've got to get to shore. Can you swim?"

"Since I was three," he bragged.

The bravado reassured her but only a little. He was weak and cold and probably near to becoming hypothermic, as she might be also. They struck out for shore. It was a pathetic tag-team effort. He pulled her when she could not go one stroke farther, and she anchored them in place as best she could when he had to stop and rest.

By the grace of God they made it, hauling each other, gasping and exhausted, onto the rocky beach.

They lay on their backs for what seemed like an eternity, their whole bodies focused on the precious act of breathing. Cast up like driftwood on the beach, exhaustion rendered them heedless of the waves that broke at their feet and the rocks that poked into their hips and shoulders. She rolled over and tucked herself next to him. He turned to curl her in the circle of his body, and though there was no warmth, she felt exquisite pleasure knowing they had both survived. Overhead the clouds were thicker than before, another spate of rain beginning to spatter down on them. She knew she'd never before seen and would never again see such a beautiful sky as this.

A rumble of thunder cracked the night, and Sarah sat up, her mind recovered enough to turn to practical matters, though her limbs were still half-dead from the swim and every muscle in her arms ached. Shelter.

Jett could not stay out here at the mercy of the elements, waiting for Beretta's men to show up. Racking her brains, she considered their options. They could not return to the house, of course, and the motorboat was gone wherever Ellsworth had taken it. The larger boat would provide shelter, but the moment she powered it up, they would give away their location, and she did not know how to operate such a large vessel by herself anyway. In Jett's exhausted condition, he might not be of much help. Maybe the boat's radio? Could they send a message? She wasn't sure, but Jett was shivering now, though he was trying not to, his teeth chattering.

At the far end of the dock was a small wooden shed, a storehouse or an office perhaps. It would have to do, at least for a while.

"Come on," she said, helping Jett to his feet. "We're

going to that shed." He wobbled and almost fell, and her own legs weren't much better, but she got a shoulder under him and they staggered to the little structure.

The door was locked. Jett braced himself against the wall, but she could tell his knees were shaking as she tore a corner from a plastic no-trespassing sign and ripped off a piece. Sliding it into the vertical crack between the door and the jamb, she jimmied the lock open.

Jett was grinning widely at her. "Where did you learn to do that?"

"Nursing school."

"Didn't know they covered breaking and entering."

"They don't, officially, but sometimes the door to the break room would accidentally lock, so it was a handy skill. We all learned how to break in when we needed to."

He laughed softly as she helped him inside.

The interior could not have been more than ten by ten, cluttered with a file drawer, a messy desk and rolling office chair. But it was safe for the moment and dry, and to her it could not have felt more palatial. Easing him to the floor was a relief to both of them. She did not dare to flip on the lights, but she found a flashlight in the top desk drawer. Keeping the beam low so it would not be detected through the window, she shone it around the cluttered space.

"Aha," she cried out in triumph.

"What? Did you find a phone?"

"No," she said, beaming. "But it's almost as good. It's a space heater." She put the little machine on full blast and aimed it right at Jett. Though she wanted nothing more than to sit down next to him and soak in the feeble warmth, she continued her prowling, coming up with two sets of oil-stained blue coveralls. She helped Jett strip off his sodden T-shirt and turned her back while he pulled on the coveralls and she did the same. The garment was made for a big man, so the material almost swallowed her up. It smelled of sweat, but at least it was dry.

Jett looked better, and his shivering had slowed. Still she insisted he remain next to the heater while she poked through every nook and cranny in the office. There were files crammed with papers, a few office supplies, but no radio of any kind and no landline.

Jett seemed lost in thought. "I was wondering what's going on at the house." He pointed to his ankle. "This thing could still be working. They're designed to be waterproof. If Tom has been able to hold out against Beretta's men, he can still track my whereabouts. We should split up."

"No."

"You go to the boat," Jett said, his voice a little stronger. "There will be a radio aboard. Call for help and lock yourself in until it arrives."

"We're staying together."

"Sarah," he said catching her hand, his face intense. "I don't want you to die because of me."

"Jett, I left you once, a long time ago, and I'm not doing it again." Those dark eyes searched hers, and she held the gaze until it hurt too much and she looked away. There in the deep water she'd realized her feelings for him still burned far down in her heart, but she'd let him go all those years ago and he was not coming back to her. They were not the same people, not the naive teens they had been, and that youthful love was just a memory shot to the surface when she'd thought he was dead. "Not until the mission is over," she added quietly. "We stick together until we escape."

He let out a low sigh. "All right. Both of us will go to the boat, then."

"As soon as you're warmed up." To escape the sadness that still circled around her stomach, she yanked open the lower desk drawer. "Look," she crowed, holding up two chocolate bars. "They left us some candy."

His silence worried her, so she unwrapped one and handed it to him.

"Thank you," he said quietly, staring at it.

"They're not mine. Thank the office guy."

"I meant thank you for saving me from drowning," he said.

She waited, sensing he had something more to add.

"And for trying to help me see the truth."

"About what?"

He swallowed. "About God."

Her breath grew shallow, and she stared at him. "Jett?"

"All those things I said, making fun of your faith. I apologize for that." He looked around the room without seeming to be aware of his surroundings.

"It's all right. We don't have to talk about that now."

"Yes, we do. I finally understood something when I was down there underwater."

Afraid to stop the flow of words, she got on her knees next to him. "Can you tell me about it?"

Water sparkled in his still wet hair. "I'm not sure. I don't understand much right now. I don't have the right words for it."

"Then tell me what you feel."

"I feel—" he paused "—like I've been released from a prison I didn't know I was in. I feel like God did that, just now, under the water." He raised his eyes to hers. "Is that possible for someone like me to feel something like that?"

She reached for his hands and squeezed them, almost

unable to speak. "Yes." Tears crowded her vision. "Yes, it is more than possible."

"I understand now what you were trying to tell me."

"I'm so glad, Jett."

"And I'm sorry." He looked at her hand in his. "For the ways I put you down about what you believe. I ridiculed you because I didn't understand, and I felt like I was on the outside looking in."

"It's okay."

"Do you think…" He let out another sigh.

"What?"

His brow was furrowed. "I've spent so many years running away from God and mocking people who believe. Do you think He can forgive that?"

She could hardly talk for the lump in her throat. "Yes, Jett," she choked out. "He can and He does." She embraced him and cried tears of joy. God had overcome Jett's resistance, his pain, and out of the near disaster, there had come the amazing gift of grace. What a triumph. What a God.

He stroked her back, holding her close, and she was not completely sure, but she thought she felt the warmth of his tears on her neck. If they could stay there, reveling in that moment forever, she would not complain.

A sharp wave of rain against the window roused them. Reluctantly, she released him.

"Storm's worsening. I wonder how many hours until sunrise," she said.

"Not enough. Sky's already lightening. We should get to the boat."

"Okay. Eat some chocolate first."

"Yes, Nurse Sarah," he said, popping a few squares into his mouth and shoving the rest in his pocket. He pointed to a hook on the door. "Looks like they left us some rain slickers to use. Finally we'll be dressed right for the weather."

They pulled on the yellow slickers and grabbed the flashlight. A sizzle of lightning shone through the window, and the following thunder sounded like a bomb deploying.

He got to his feet with only a slight wobble, closing his eyes for a moment.

"Are you okay?"

"'Course," he said. "I live for this stuff."

"Right." She stayed close anyway in case his body could not live up to his mouth.

He reached for the door handle. "Ready?"

She gave herself only a second to consider what had transpired. She'd believed him dead, anguished at his loss, rejoiced at his return and shared in his acceptance of God. How was it all possible?

It was more than possible with God, she thought.

She gave him a nod. "I'm ready."

He yanked the door open.

Standing outside, an evil grin on his face and Tom's phone in his hand, was Beretta's goon, Miguel.

"*Hola*, American," he said. "Good to see you again."

SIXTEEN

Miguel, Beretta's sadistic right-hand man, was dressed for the elements in a waterproof camo outfit and heavy boots. This time he had a knife fastened to his belt and a pistol instead of the baseball bat. He clipped Jett on the shoulder with the butt of his gun, sending rivers of pain along Jett's side. Apparently, the guy still held a grudge.

"Get going, American," he jeered. "I'd love the excuse to kill you right now."

Jett was no longer dizzy, but his body still felt the accumulated effects of nearly drowning and hypothermia. Yet there remained an inexplicable warmth in his system. What had passed between him and Sarah in the shed was something precious, he knew. He'd shared the most wondrous thing that had ever happened to him with her, the woman who had both loved and hurt him. Now they were about to be marched off to meet Beretta's men and face a new set of horrors, but whatever happened, he knew he would treasure that sliver of time that had changed his life and his afterlife forever.

Miguel jerked him from his thoughts by shoving them both into the front of a golf cart parked under a fringe of Torrey pines.

"You drive, American," Miguel said, pressing his gun hard into Jett's neck. "It's time to go meet Senor Beretta."

"Great," Jett said. "I've been looking forward to it."

"So has he," Miguel said with a hard laugh.

Sarah sat beside him, head held high, though he knew she must be disappointed to the point of defeat. He wanted to reach for her hand, but he was afraid Miguel would strike out and hurt Sarah.

The sun was rising, cutting through the heavy cloud cover. Morning. They'd made it to morning, somehow.

One hour at a time, Sarah. Just hang on a little while longer. Every moment they stayed alive was a victory, he told himself as he guided the cart to the rear of the house. All they had to do was survive until Marco and the Gallaghers could convince the cops to get a search warrant.

There was no outward damage to the structure that Jett could see. If he hadn't known what had gone on the past few hours, he would have seen no evidence of it from the exterior. Miguel ordered them through the back door and into the same formal dining room where they had recently been taken by Ellsworth. Tom was there, hands bound behind his back, and Mr. Ellsworth—who appeared perfectly calm in a fresh suit and loafers—sat at the table, hands free. He looked as though he was completely in charge of the situation.

"Mr. Ellsworth," Sarah said without preamble, voice vibrating with outrage, "you left us to die."

He arched an eyebrow. "I needed to return to the mansion. It was very cold."

Cold? Jett and Sarah locked eyes. There was something hideously wrong with Ezra Ellsworth, and whether he knew it or not, he was no longer anywhere near in control of the situation.

"Where is Del Young?" she demanded.

"He's alive," Tom said. "He's like a cat. Always ends up on his feet."

A dark-haired man with a barrel chest, wearing khaki cargo pants and a rain slicker, stood next to the gas fireplace, smoking a cigarette with one arm thrown carelessly over the mantel. Antonio Beretta's close-cropped beard was neatly trimmed, glasses accentuating his deep-set eyes.

Through a wisp of cigarette smoke, Beretta looked them over, glancing at Sarah and studying Jett with more attention.

"You fight well," he said in perfect English.

"I'm flattered."

"Our visit here in the States will be short. We do not wish to attract attention."

"Then it was probably a mistake to shoot down the helicopter," Jett suggested. "Not exactly subtle."

Beretta waved a weary hand. "Miguel is too exuberant."

"Miguel is stupid."

Miguel took a step toward Jett, mouth twisted in rage, but Beretta stopped him and chuckled. "Perhaps, but Alex tells me the wreck is now completely submerged, and the storm, well, it will also help to help conceal the accident, so no harm done."

"It wasn't an accident," Sarah said, "and there was great harm done. Miguel murdered the pilot and nearly killed the rest of us."

Beretta ignored her. "I wish to have my painting returned. This man—" he pointed to Ellsworth "—hired Del Young to steal it from me, but Young has double-crossed him and hidden the painting."

"The security on your compound needs improvement," Jett said.

"It has been improved." Beretta's eyes glittered. "Those

guards are no longer alive." He looked at Sarah. "I had my man search Young's apartment in Los Angeles. *The Red Lady* was not there, but he did run into your people."

Sarah's head jerked up. "My people?"

"Your sisters and a man."

Jett saw the hope flare up in her face and knew it matched his own. Marco and the Gallaghers were searching for them—they'd figured out the Del Young connection.

"You'd better let us go then, before the police arrive to arrest you," she said.

"There is not enough of a trail to lead them to me," Beretta said. "I will be gone before there are any further complications."

"Maybe not," Tom said. "The cops called here already, asking to speak to Mr. Ellsworth."

Beretta lifted a careless shoulder. "Did Young disclose to you where he hid my painting, Nurse?"

"My name is Sarah, and no, he didn't. He said he could not remember."

"A lie, perhaps?"

"It could be the truth, since your people caused him a grievous head injury." She shot a contemptuous look at Miguel.

"As I said, overexuberant. They were meant to capture him and make him talk, but he is not a strong man." The derision in Beretta's tone was clear. "He is in the upstairs hospital room. We will find out the answer from him after you wake him."

"What if I can't?"

The look he gave her was so cold that Jett wanted to step in between them.

"You will wake him," he said softly. "Or you both will die."

While Ellsworth maintained the facade of a gentleman, Beretta did not even try. He was a killer, plain and simple, and he pretended nothing else. Jett knew their time was running out.

Miguel was gesturing with his gun for Sarah and Jett to head upstairs when Alex appeared, jacket wet from the rain. He whispered something in Beretta's ear. The drug lord's eyes narrowed, giving him a reptilian look.

"We have attracted attention after all," he said. "The harbor patrol is here to ask some questions, even though they were told that Ellsworth was not at home when they called earlier."

Jett's heart leaped. Finally. It was probably Marco's doing. "They know something is going on here. Looks like you've got some explaining to do, Beretta."

Beretta's smile did not reassure Jett.

"I will explain nothing," he said, turning to Alex and Miguel. "Take them."

There wasn't time to return Jett and Sarah to their cells before the harbor patrol officer began to hammer on the door. Sarah tried to scream, but Alex fastened a hand firmly across her lips.

Alex and Miguel dragged them into a room halfway down the hall and secured their mouths with duct tape. It was a small library with floor-to-ceiling shelves of books and a grouping of leather chairs.

"No noise," Alex cautioned, leaving the door cracked so he could hear the situation developing below. They were close enough to catch the conversation drifting up from the front foyer. Sarah scanned the room for something with which she could make noise, attract attention. Jett was doing the same, she guessed. Her nerves were tingling with excitement. She recognized the voice of one of the cops, Officer Ridley from her own town of Coronado. Marco and her sisters had been pulling strings.

Tom spoke in a cool, friendly tone. They'd no doubt ordered him to get rid of the cops as quickly as possible.

"Mr. Ellsworth is not in residence. He's at his home in Brussels. I can give you the number, if you'd like, but he very rarely communicates by phone. I am the only employee on the property right now. We sent the others home early this morning due to the storm."

"We are looking for two people, Sarah Gallagher and Dominic Jett. They were abducted from a clinic in Mexico four days ago," Ridley said. "Ms. Gallagher's family operates a detective agency, and they believe the two were transported here from Mexico."

Sarah's heart beat faster. They knew. Finally, things were starting to go their way.

"I'm sorry to hear about the abduction, but I don't see how it could possibly connect to Mr. Ellsworth."

"Sarah Gallagher sent a message to her sister from this area."

They'd gotten her email. She could hardly breathe.

"Are you saying it was sent from this house?"

Tom was a cool customer. There was just the right note of incredulity in his voice.

"We can't say that specifically," the cop said, "but it originated in the Santa Barbara region. Do you mind if we check your computers?"

Proof. They would be found now and rescued. She forced herself to take a breath through her nose as the seconds ticked by.

"Actually yes, Officers, I do mind. Mr. Ellsworth is a particularly private man. A person of his resources has to be careful with information." He paused. "Feel free to return with a warrant, if you'd like to pursue this line of questioning, but it's a waste of your time, I'm afraid."

Her stomach bunched in agony. *No*, she wanted to scream. *We're right here.* She eyed a small table, home to a porcelain vase. Miguel and Alex were listening intently to the conversation. She edged closer to the table. A flicker of understanding crossed Jett's face as he intuited her intent.

"Do you know of a man named Del Young?" the cops continued.

Tom paused. "I don't believe so."

"Marco Quidel, who works with the Gallaghers, interviewed a mechanic who worked on your Jet Skis, and he said Young was staying here on the island."

Try to lie your way out of that one. Sarah eased forward another inch.

"Oh, now I remember. Yes, he was here on and off as a guest of Mary Ellsworth. I haven't seen him for about three months, I'd say. Do you suspect him of being involved with the two missing people?"

The officers answered, but Sarah was too focused on her plan to pay attention. She was almost close enough to kick out and send the table and vase crashing to the ground.

"All right," Officer Ridley was saying. "We'll call you if we have any further questions, and we'll be contacting your boss in Brussels. Thank you for your time."

She could hear them moving toward the door. It was now or never.

"Thank you for coming by, gentlemen," Tom was saying.

Sarah kicked out, striking the table and sending it over. The vase tumbled exactly as she'd hoped, heading for a hard landing on the ceramic tile floor.

Alex lunged forward to catch it, but Jett stepped in

his way, hooking an ankle and causing Alex to stumble.
It was the few seconds they needed.

The vase hit the floor, fracturing into pieces, sending bits of porcelain skittering across the tile. Alex and
Miguel each grabbed a prisoner, yanking them close and
pulling their pistols.

Her heart thudded. They had heard. How could they
not? They would come. Surely Miguel and Alex would
not risk shooting them dead with officers right outside.
Rescue. It was so close she could taste it.

"What was that?" Ridley asked. "I thought you were
the only employee here."

The seconds seemed to tick by in slow motion. "It's
the cat, I'm afraid. She's been trouble since the day Mr.
Ellsworth purchased her, but he has a soft spot for the
animal."

"A cat?"

"Yes." Another pause. "You can see her water bowl
and food dish there in the foyer. More trouble than she's
worth, that's for sure."

No, no, no, Sarah's mind screamed. She strained in
Alex's grip, but his fingers bit into her wrists. She could
picture Tom's smug smile. The cops could not search
the house unless they had reason to believe lives were
in danger.

We're here, she screamed behind the duct tape.

Alex shook her so hard her head snapped back.
"Quiet," he hissed.

"All right. Thank you for your time," came the voices
from downstairs. There was a shuffle of feet, the click
of the latch.

No, don't leave, she pleaded silently. *Don't leave us
here.*

And then the door closed on their hope of escape.

SEVENTEEN

Sarah felt limp and as wrung out as an old dishrag. They'd been within inches of their rescuers, but in a blink they were forced back in their cages in the wine cellar, waiting for their captors to bring them to the ailing Del Young.

The hours stretched on and on, interrupted by the howl of the storm. She felt like howling, too, the disappointment almost too heavy to bear. Jett tried to comfort her, but she was too depleted to do anything but flop onto the cot and roll herself in the thin blanket.

She eventually drifted to sleep, dozing in fits and starts, awakening disoriented. Her prison was silent, and for a terrifying moment she imagined Jett was gone, that they'd taken him while she slept, or that he had not been strong enough to endure the cold and lack of food after his near drowning. "Jett?" she whispered.

"Right here," he said, calming her.

"What time is it?"

"Not sure exactly. Sometime in the wee hours of Sunday morning."

She sank back onto her cot, the emotions circling and biting at her like ravenous sharks. Another day, still caged like an animal with little hope of rescue. The futility of it all crushed her. Hiding her face in the blankets, she tried not to cry.

Jett stood, forearms resting on the bars. "Sarah Gal, I hear sniffling. You're not giving up, are you?"

The words almost loosened a flood of crying, but she bit it back. "It's just that we were so close and I'm tired, Jett. Everything we attempt comes to nothing. We've been tied up, threatened and almost killed by a falling helicopter. I mean, who has that happen to them?"

He chuckled. "Yeah, that's one for the books, all right."

"I just want it to be over."

"If the police came here thinking Ellsworth is hiding something, Marco knows, too, and he's not going to stop until he finds us."

She clung to his words. "My sisters won't, either."

"Are they good detectives?"

"Yes, and they're even better sisters."

"That much I knew. They were pretty protective of you—the ones I met anyway."

"Yes, but we're running out of time. I don't know how much longer I can keep hoping."

He paused. "Remember when you decided the high school needed a rose garden? It was right before we split up."

She groaned. "Oh, yeah. I planted a half dozen rose-bushes, Mr. Lincolns. They were gorgeous hybrid tea roses, and vandals promptly dug them up and stole them."

"Three times."

"Uh-huh. Took all my money to keep replacing them, even with the discount the man at the garden store gave me because he felt so sorry for me. It was a stupid thing to do, because the groundskeepers eventually dug out the roses anyway to expand the gym. I bought eighteen

Mr. Lincolns and there's still not one rose anywhere on that campus."

"But the thing is, you kept planting—that's the important part, and the third time, the vandals gave up."

She looked at him, heart aching at the memory. "You laughed at me back then, Jett. You and your buddies." How his guffaws had cut right to her heart, made her feel foolish, small and worthless.

"Yeah. I did, and I'm very sorry about that." His tone dropped. "I was hurt, angry that you broke up with me, and I acted like a child." He sighed. "But secretly, I thought you had grit to keep planting those roses."

Grit. She hadn't known of his admiration, only his ridicule. Her cheeks warmed. "That was right before you got into that last brawl on campus."

"Short fuse. No excuse."

"And after we...after I broke up with you, you dropped out, without a word to me or anyone else. Why didn't you talk to a counselor or social worker or someone?"

In the dim light, she could see him rest his forehead against the metal that caged him. "I didn't trust anyone after you were gone."

No, she thought. It went deeper than that. Did she have the courage to say it now? To air the painful inkling that she'd buried down deep the past nine years? What had she to lose, except maybe to ruin the intimacy they'd achieved through their ordeal? It was time to drum up the confidence to say aloud what her heart had whispered for so long. She took a deep breath. "Before that, Jett. You didn't trust me fully even before that."

His head jerked up. "I trusted you, Sarah, more than anyone."

"You shared the good stuff with me. You were the fun guy, the happy-go-lucky Dominic Jett, the cool kid always looking for a laugh. But you didn't trust me with your pain. I had hints about your father, but you never talked openly about him or the abuse."

He was quiet for a moment. "I thought if you saw what my life was like, you wouldn't want me anymore."

"How could you believe that?"

His fingers closed around the bars. "You had this perfect family and you talked about God all the time. Why would someone like you want to be with a guy from my messed-up world?"

She'd thought the hurt of losing Jett had died, but just then it surged back, as intense as it ever had been. "I wanted to be with you because I loved you. Loving means taking the bad stuff, too."

From somewhere in the cellar came the drip of water, slow and regular, marking the moments of their captivity in meticulous measure.

"I thought if you knew, I'd lose you. Ironic, because I lost you anyway."

She clutched the blanket tighter. "I called, I wrote, message after message. When you saw me in town, you'd walk the other way." Her voice trembled. "Like I was something disgusting for you to look at."

"Sarah…" His voice broke. "If I made you feel like that, I'm lower than pond scum. I didn't see how I was hurting you." He banged his hand against the bars. "That's not honest. Yes, I did see, and I wanted it. I wanted to hurt you, to punish you for dumping me. I was about to explode with all the anger inside me. My dad went to jail around then. It's probably the only reason I didn't completely self-destruct."

"Your mother finally pressed charges?"

He laughed, soft and bitter. "No. My mother never pressed charges against my father, even when he broke her arm. It was always her fault, she'd say—she'd done something wrong, provoked him. It drove me completely crazy."

"So what happened?"

"That time, the time he broke her arm, I called the police and she denied he hurt her, giving them some story about falling on the patio. When they left, my dad tried to punish me for calling the cops, only he got out his handgun that time."

Her breath shallowed out. "Oh, Jett."

"Fortunately, he shot me instead of her. Took a piece out of my shoulder, but it was enough to arrest him. He's in jail for fifteen years. My mother moved in with her sister in Laguna Beach, but I refused to go, and I was eighteen so she couldn't force me. I hope she stays there. My aunt is good for her."

She could hardly push out the words. "Jett, why didn't you tell me? I could have helped—listened, at least, and prayed for you."

For an instant, his expression was that of a stricken teen again. "How could I go back to school, to you, and face that? Tough kid like me is not gonna return to classes and admit to everyone his dad's in jail for shooting him and his mom's moved away. I was living in my truck, sneaking into the corner gym at night to shower and eating the free samples at the grocery store for food. No way I could let everyone find out."

"Jett," she whispered, eyes damp thinking about his misery, his shame.

He cleared his throat. "That's how Marco came into my life. He realized the situation that I didn't want anyone to see." His voice dropped to a whisper. "That I didn't want you to see."

She stood, fingers clutching the bars, allowing his pain

to wash over her. What could she say? Nothing. There were no words to ease over the disastrous past. All she could do was listen now, as she hadn't been able to do then. "It would have been okay—to show me, I mean. To tell me what you were going through."

He was quiet for a long time, and she knew he was reliving that dark time, the shock, the betrayal he'd experienced when she walked away. How lonely he must have felt. Marco had been, and still was, she suspected, his lifeline.

Jett's voice sounded faint and hollow, as if he was a very long way away. "You always talked about God, how He was your protector and savior, and I wondered why He didn't protect and save me. I figured He only helped people like you, and that made me angry, too."

Each word cut like a scalpel. If only they had had this conversation then, how different things might have been for Jett. At that moment, she understood she'd been the only person allowed into Jett's heart and how very badly she'd scarred him by leaving.

He sighed. "I'm sorry, Sarah."

"I'm sorry, too. I'm sorry that I came across as that girl from the perfect family who couldn't understand. I should have listened more. I liked the fun Dominic Jett. The cool kid that everyone respected. Maybe I didn't work hard enough to fully know you because I didn't want to see the difficult things." She knew it was true as she spoke the words. *God, forgive me.*

"You did your best under the circumstances. Anyway, that was a long time ago. I grew up, found a career and lost it." The water continued to drip, marking the seconds of silence. "I'll get it together now. Settle down."

She tried a smile. "White-picket-fence kind of settle down?"

He laughed. "Nah. I'm not marriage material." He paused. "But I hope you find someone great, because you deserve it."

You are great, Jett.

With what he'd learned and experienced these last few days, he was different, as if he'd finally been given permission to put down an impossible burden. She loved the Jett she had lost, and she rejoiced about the man he'd become. God was doing something special in Dominic Jett, and she was sad that she would not be around to see how he would blossom if they survived Ellsworth and Beretta. They could never be together.

They'd hurt each other too much.

Her heart was still flayed wide from her father's death.

And Jett didn't want a second chance with her, either—that much was clear as he stepped back and sat down on his cot.

Grief and joy mixed together in her heart, and she marveled again that the two feelings could live side by side. The gulf between her and Jett remained, but at least he now understood that he mattered to God, that he'd mattered all along.

From somewhere above them, a door slammed. At any moment, she knew, they would be summoned. Beretta would not hesitate to kill them when they were no longer useful.

Death and life, she thought. *How close together they are.*

She folded her hands and prayed.

Jett allowed himself to doze, partially to renew his depleted energy and partly to escape the bombardment of memories and past pain. What if he'd opened up to Sarah about his shame when they were back in high school?

He likely never would have hit bottom and then felt God's push propelling him up toward the surface again, allowing him his first deep breath of peace. No, the pain had been worth it. Sarah was a part of his troubled past and twined around his promise of a better future. Yesterday and tomorrow, there would always be a piece of his heart that belonged to her. She deserved a long and brilliant life, and he prayed she would get it.

Let me get her out of here, Lord. Show me the way to save her.

It seemed he had just drifted off when the door squeaked open and Alex and Miguel pushed Tom into the room.

"Let them out," Miguel demanded.

Tom unlocked the cells. His expression told Jett the situation. This was it. They had no more options. The muscles deep in his stomach tightened the way they did when he would approach an explosive device. The remaining moments of their safety were ticking away in triple time. He wanted to reach for Sarah's hand, but Alex moved her forward and Miguel took position behind Jett and Tom.

They were taken to another bedroom, and this time Young was tied to the bedposts.

"This isn't necessary," Sarah protested. "He's injured. He doesn't need to be bound."

"We have no time for him to jump out any more windows," Alex said. "We heard he is prone to such desperate acts."

Not anymore, Jett thought. Young appeared to have reached his physical limits.

Beretta entered, still smoking.

"Put that out," Sarah demanded.

He laughed. "Are you worried the smoke will make him sick?"

Miguel and Alex joined in the laughter.

"Don't you have any human decency?" she snapped.

Beretta waved the cigarette at Young. "Talk to him, Nurse. Make him tell you."

"I told you, my name is Sarah."

Beretta gave her a steely look. "I grow weary of your attitude. Do as you're told."

Cheeks flaming, Sarah moved to Young and did a quick exam. Jett knew enough to suspect that her diagnosis would not be encouraging. He wasn't surprised when she finished and turned to face Beretta with a dire expression. "He's short of breath and there's abdominal swelling. He could be bleeding internally. He's been lying here without medical attention for hours."

"Make him talk," Beretta repeated.

Her eyes were wide with exasperation. "He's been in a helicopter crash. He can't talk."

"Yes, he can. He's been babbling for an hour. Tom's been writing down everything he said." Beretta gestured to Tom, who handed over a paper. Beretta waved it in front of her. "Something about lookout and a vacation. It means nothing. I need more and I won't wait any longer. Ask him."

Sarah's face was taut with emotion. Jett yearned to do something to help her.

She bent over Young and took his hand. "Mr. Young? Can you hear me?"

He wriggled a little as if to find a more comfortable position, but his forehead was lined with pain, beads of sweat on his cheeks. His skin was milk pale. Jett had the sinking feeling he was looking at a man standing on the brink of death.

"He needs a hospital," Sarah snapped at Beretta.

"He needs to talk," Beretta replied. "Now."

"I won't force him."

"You will, or I will have Miguel persuade him."

Her mouth tightened, and she turned to her patient again. "Mr. Young, can you hear me?" Sarah said.

Young's eyes opened. He looked dazed, disoriented.

"It's Sarah Gallagher," she said, stroking his hand. "I've been trying to help you."

"Sarah?" he whispered. "The detective?"

She smiled. "I've been your nurse, mostly."

Young's other hand grasped hers in a white-knuckle grip. "I loved her. I was never good enough for her."

"Who?"

"Mary."

Jett saw Tom tense.

"Where is Mary, Mr. Young? We're trying to find her."

"Ask about *The Red Lady*," Beretta demanded, "or I'll ask him myself."

Tears began to leak down Young's face. "I'm sorry. It never should have happened."

"Where?" Sarah pressed. "Where is she? We need to go find her and help her."

"Where is *The Red Lady*?" Beretta said, pushing his way to the bed.

Young shrank back as far as he could against the blankets and started to cry.

Sarah shot Beretta a look that would have melted steel in a less ruthless man. "You're upsetting him. Let me ask the questions, why don't you?"

Beretta clenched his jaw.

"Mr. Young," she said again in a gentle tone, "can you tell me where you hid Mary and the painting?"

"Got to find her," he groaned, thrashing on the bed.

"It's okay," she said, trying to soothe him. She looked

at Beretta. "Please let me get him to the hospital. I'm begging you. He's in pain."

"Ask him," Beretta roared.

Sarah jumped, breathing hard. Jett moved toward her, but Miguel pointed the pistol at him.

She looked at Beretta for a long moment, and then she looked at Jett. She'd come to some sort of decision. *Whatever it is*, he tried to tell her with a slight nod, *whatever you need to do, I will back you up.*

Forever, his heart finished, even though he knew she no longer belonged to him.

Sarah turned back to Young and leaned close, using a damp cloth to sponge away the sweat from his forehead. He relaxed against the sheets.

"Mr. Young," she said, stroking his face. "Do you know that God loves you?"

Jett's breath hitched.

"No," Beretta snarled, "that is not what you're talking about."

Sarah ignored him.

Young looked at her intently, his eyes clearing for a moment. "I have been a bad person."

She leaned closer. "God forgives, and He loves you. He has overcome the world and He is stronger than death."

In that moment, he knew he'd never see a more magnificent gesture as Sarah looked away from the precarious present and tried to point a fallen man toward the comfort of eternity.

Beretta reached past Sarah and grabbed Young by the shoulders. "Enough," he yelled, shaking him. "You will tell me what I want to know."

Sarah tried to pull Beretta off, and Miguel reached for her, but Jett knocked him out of the way, sending Miguel's pistol flying. Recovering, Miguel and Alex dived on Jett, attempting to pin him to the floor. Jett struggled with everything in him. From the corner of his eye, he saw Tom wrench a cell phone from Miguel's back pocket and sprint for the door.

"Alex, get Tom," Beretta shouted. "He's going for Ellsworth."

Alex sprang to his feet and headed off in pursuit.

Miguel and Jett continued to wrestle. Miguel was strong, but Jett was fueled by a ferocious desire for victory. Ignoring the buzzing in his ears and the agony in his muscles, Jett finally forced Miguel facedown on the floor, his knee between the man's shoulders. He was pulling off Miguel's belt to fasten his hands behind his back when a shot exploded through the room.

Beretta stood with his pistol aimed upward, bits of plaster drifting down from where his bullet had plowed into the ceiling. "Stop," he shouted, spittle flying from his mouth.

Jett stepped back, breathing hard, and Miguel rose. He snapped out a punch at Jett that connected with his cheekbone, making him see sparks and almost sending him to the floor. Miguel was going to follow up with another blow when Beretta stopped him.

"If I don't get what I want," he hissed, "I will shoot you all dead where you stand."

Sarah looked up from the bed, tears streaming down her face. "Then I guess you better start shooting, because Mr. Young is dead."

EIGHTEEN

Sarah gently pulled the sheet over Del Young's face and whispered a final prayer for him. Anguish washed through her insides at what the man had endured. At least he'd felt God's comfort in his final moments. Beretta was pacing the room like a caged tiger, but she did not give him the satisfaction of her attention. The coward, the greedy, brutal coward.

She should be afraid, she knew, but instead she was seething. Beretta had no reason to keep them alive now and murder was surely on his mind, but she felt only rage that Beretta and Ellsworth had let Del Young suffer in his final hours instead of getting him the medical help he needed.

"Nurse," Beretta called.

Sarah felt her self-control snap like a rubber band. "Stop calling me that. My name is Sarah Gallagher and this man—" she gestured to Del Young "—this man had a name, too."

"This man," Beretta said, face twisted with disgust, "stole from me. He was a thief."

"And you are in no position to judge him," she said. "You intimidate people and traffic in the drug trade.

You are a criminal and a thug, far worse than Del Young ever was."

Beretta sent the small tray with medical supplies crashing to the floor. Sarah flinched. Jett tried to step between Beretta and Sarah, but Miguel held him tight.

"You are nothing, Nurse. Your opinion means nothing. I have done great things for my community, my villagers. To them I am a hero."

"They don't respect you," Jett put in. "They fear you."

"I am their benefactor."

Sarah shook her head. "No, a benefactor loves the people he helps. You only love yourself."

Beretta spat, the saliva splatting onto the floor at her feet. It was all she could do to stand her ground.

"And you are a worthless woman who has learned to speak too much."

Sarah raised her chin and looked him right in the face. "You let this man die in agony when you could have shown compassion. That tells me all I need to know about you."

Beretta's chest was heaving, mouth contorted. She thought he was going to strike out at her. Jett must have thought so, too, because he strained against Miguel's hold. Whatever the drug lord had been about to do, he was interrupted when Alex returned to murmur in his ear. The report sent him into a tirade of angry Spanish as Sarah listened in.

"So Ellsworth and Tom have escaped?" she said. "My goodness, you do have trouble keeping track of your prisoners, don't you?"

Now it was Jett sending her a *don't poke the bear* look, but she was past caring.

"You won't get what you want now. You've wasted all this time and left two men dead, and you've got nothing. Your painting will remain hidden wherever Young stashed it. Or maybe Mary Ellsworth will go sell it on her own, or even better, she'll give it back to her father."

Beretta was breathing in short angry bursts.

"Sarah," Jett warned.

"Wouldn't that be ironic?" she said. "If Ellsworth wound up with *The Red Lady* in the end in spite of everything you've done to get it back?"

"He will not have my painting," Beretta said through gritted teeth.

"They might be on their way to pick it up right now. Maybe Tom understood Young's ramblings and knows perfectly well where he hid the painting. He was waiting for a chance to get away, and he got one while you were here playing the part of the bully."

Beretta raised his gun, and Jett broke free of Miguel and leaped between them. "We can still find *The Red Lady* for you."

Beretta's finger tightened on the trigger, and he lifted the weapon to pin Sarah in his sights over Jett's shoulder.

"Talk," he demanded.

"The list," he said, talking fast. "The words Tom recorded. They're clues to where Young stashed *The Red Lady*."

Beretta's eyes narrowed. "They could be delirious babble."

"Give Sarah a chance to look it over. She's a detective. She can figure it out."

Sarah had no idea what Jett hoped to accomplish by bringing that into the conversation, but she stayed silent, trying to calm her raging pulse.

"A girl detective?" Beretta laughed. "It is too bad I am not in the mood for humor."

"It's not a joke. She works for Pacific Coast Investigations with her family. Those are the people your man ran into at Del Young's apartment."

Beretta raised a thick eyebrow and jutted his chin at Miguel, who brought up something on his cell phone.

"'Pacific Coast Investigations,'" Beretta read from the screen. "'Associate Sarah Gallagher.'" He laughed long and loud. "And to think, I believed I was talking to Florence Nightingale, and instead I have a Dick Tracy in my presence. Or perhaps a Nancy Drew? My daughters like to read of this American girl detective. Is that who you are trying to be, Nurse?"

Miguel pocketed the phone. "It doesn't matter. They cannot find the painting. This is a ruse to distract you."

"I am inclined to agree with you, Miguel." Beretta's finger tightened a fraction more. "I cannot leave behind witnesses to what has gone on here. Bodies, yes. Witnesses, no."

"But what have you got to lose?" Jett said. "She's right. At the moment you have nothing but a mess here on Ellsworth Island. A couple more hours might mean the difference between getting your painting back and leaving empty-handed."

Miguel's eyes blazed hatred at Jett. "The longer we stay here, the more likely the police will become a problem. We should kill them and go, now."

"Empty-handed," Jett repeated. "Never knowing how close you were to retrieving your painting.

"Not totally empty-handed," Miguel said. "We will be able to kill you two. That's something to take satisfaction in, anyway."

Beretta was thinking it over, the gun still aimed. He was cruel, but Sarah was praying that his sense of greed outweighed his brutality.

"Let her look," Jett prompted. "If there's a chance

she can get *The Red Lady* back, you'd be foolish not to let her try."

"They're desperate," Miguel said. "They are stalling to save their skins, that is all."

Beretta's eyes moved from Jett to the shrouded man on the bed. The seconds passed.

"Think of *The Red Lady*, your priceless painting out there somewhere, hidden," he prompted.

"Don't believe them," Miguel said.

"Quiet." Stroking his beard, he turned to Sarah. "How will you figure out this puzzle?"

Jett heard Sarah gulp. "I… I need to make one phone call, to my sisters at the agency."

Beretta laughed. "You take me for a fool, Nurse Sarah. Would you like to dial the police, too, while you're at it?"

"I will use any phone you like. You can listen to every word."

"Why would I let you involve them?"

She thought fast. "Because they were there in Del Young's apartment. They might have seen something that will explain these words—a trip he was planning, a destination where he stowed *The Red Lady*."

The room grew so silent Sarah could practically hear her own heart thudding a frantic staccato in his chest. Their only hope was that Beretta's desire to retrieve his painting would outweigh his caution.

After a moment, Beretta came to a decision. "You are persuasive, Nurse, but I am not convinced." He aimed the gun and fired.

Jett heard the whistle of the bullet and Sarah's scream as the shot passed between them and buried itself in the plaster wall. His body ricocheted with terror as he reacted to the bullet missing her by mere inches.

Sarah's hands were clapped over her ears and he scrambled to her, making sure the shot had not hit her. Her whole body was trembling, and tears sparkled on her cheeks.

Rage filled him to overflowing as he turned to Beretta, who was laughing heartily.

"You see?" Beretta said. "I am a criminal thug with a sense of humor. You should see your faces."

Jett held Sarah's shaking shoulders, pulling her to his side, not taking his eyes off Beretta. *I'm going to see you brought down if it takes my very last breath to do it.*

Still chuckling, Beretta gestured to Miguel with a jerk of the head. Miguel stared daggers at Jett and Sarah, but he freed the phone from his pocket.

"It's a burner phone, paid for with cash and disposable. Your people at the agency will not be able to trace it, if that was your intent. Tell Miguel the number, and he will dial for you."

"This is a mistake," Miguel hissed. "They are manipulating you."

"If they attempt to identify me or give away this location," Beretta said mildly, "they will be dead before the phone hits the floor along with their bodies."

That gave Miguel a sneer of satisfaction.

Sarah recited the number and Miguel dialed, thrusting the phone at Sarah, who took it with trembling fingers.

"H-hello?" she said. Tears sprang in her eyes, and Jett knew she'd heard her sister's voice.

Beretta waved his gun. "Put it on speaker. Now."

Candace's voice filled the room. "Sarah," she sobbed. "Where are you? Are you all right? We've been going crazy."

"Yes, I'm all right for now. You're on speakerphone with me and Jett."

Marco came on the line. "Are you hurt?"

"No."

"Tell me your location right now."

Beretta gave her warning look.

"I can't do that."

Marco paused. "There are people holding you there, listening to this conversation?"

"Yes, and don't bother tracing the number. It's a burner phone."

"Jett, you there?" Marco asked.

"Yes, sir."

"Unharmed?"

"For the most part."

"All right," Marco said, voice low and dangerous, "whoever you are, holding Sarah and Jett, listen to me very carefully. I'm going to find you, and if you hurt either one of them in any way, you will spend the rest of your life wishing you hadn't."

Jett's insides tightened at Marco's quiet ferocity. If Beretta didn't comply, he was going to realize their mistake the hard way. He'd once seen Marco track for a hundred miles a man he'd witnessed abusing and robbing an elderly clerk at a gas station. The guy had been relieved to be handed over to the cops after Marco brought him in. Jett knew part of Marco's strategy was to get Beretta talking so he could gain more intel on his enemy.

Beretta's mouth quirked, but he did not take the bait and remained silent. He made a hurry-up gesture.

"I need you to do something for me," Sarah said.

"Oh, Sarah, we'll do anything we can." Candace's voice quavered. "Are they treating you okay? Can you tell me that at least?"

"We're okay for the moment. Candace, I don't have

a lot of time. I need you to listen to a list of words and think about what you saw in Del Young's apartment."

"How did you know we were—" Candace started.

Sarah kept going. "Never mind that. *Lookout, vacation, spotting.* Those are the words."

"What? What are you talking about, Sarah?" Candace said.

"Del Young must have been planning some sort of trip. Can you make sense of these words? Figure out a location based on what you saw in his apartment and these clues?"

"I don't know."

"Please," Sarah pleaded. "Candace, if you don't… we—they will kill us."

"No," she breathed, undisguised panic in her voice. "No, whoever you are, please don't hurt them. We'll figure it out. What are you looking for, exactly? Tell me and we can help find what they're after."

Sarah chewed her lip. "I can't tell you that. I need a possible location, Candace. You have to hurry."

"We'll do anything you want. There's no reason to harm them," Candace said, voice throbbing with tears. "We have plenty of resources here at our disposal."

"Just the location," Sarah repeated. "Anywhere he might have been headed." She read Beretta's lips. "And if you go to the police…"

"We won't," Candace blurted. "We won't. Just don't hurt them. We'll figure out the location, I promise."

"We need time," Marco snapped. "Three hours at least to run it through the computers and analyze the photos we took at Young's place."

Beretta took the phone and covered it with his palm. "Tell him the number. He can call you back in one hour."

"But…"

"One hour," Beretta said. He handed the phone to Sarah.

She repeated the directions.

"That's not long enough," Marco said.

Would an hour be long enough for Marco and Candace to put the pieces together? Jett was not sure, but it was an hour more than they'd had before.

Beretta took the phone from her again and disconnected. The grief shimmering on Sarah's face made him want to take the legs out from under Beretta. Her family was being tortured by their kidnapping, and the phone call added both comfort and fresh agony to the situation. His only solace was that Beretta had made the fatal mistake of angering Marco Quidel. He would live to regret it, even if Jett and Sarah did not.

Beretta held out the paper to Jett. "You have one hour. During that time we will attempt to recapture Tom and Ellsworth. In the meantime, Miguel will be outside the door. If you try to leave this room, Miguel will kill you. If you or your people don't have an answer by the time I come back, I will kill you. If your family disobeys and contacts the police, they will arrive to find there is no one left alive on this island to save."

He walked out of the room.

Miguel trailed after him, stopping with a hand on the doorknob. He grinned. "It's better this way, American. You have another hour to think about your death. And I have another hour to enjoy your misery."

He slammed the door.

"That guy's really getting on my last nerve," Jett muttered.

Sarah was staring at him, mouth open. "What were you doing telling him I could find the missing painting?"

"Buying time for Marco and your sisters to locate us

or at least convince the cops to get a search warrant. Now they know we're alive, being held by someone who knows about Del Young's apartment. They'll put it together."

"But how can I figure out where *The Red Lady* is before Beretta comes back? Marco and Candace might not be able to figure it out, either. This list might not mean anything at all."

He handed her the paper. "Only one way to find out."

"I don't have any idea how to make sense of this."

"You can do it."

"But what if I can't?" she said, clutching his hands, her own skin icy cold. She was still badly shaken from Young's death, terrorized by Beretta's actions, unsure of her own abilities. She did not have the strength to believe in herself. So he would do it for her.

He gave her the old Dominic Jett grin. "Sarah Gal, you always were the smartest girl I ever knew. So put on your detective hat, and let's solve this."

NINETEEN

Sarah was on her knees, smoothing the paper on the floor with her fingers, mumbling over the strange words. Jett preferred to pace, even though he could only manage a few steps in each direction in the small room while avoiding the final resting place of Del Young. They'd both spent time praying by Young's body. He didn't know what to say—the conversation with God was something so new to him that he felt like a toddler groping for words. He let her do the out loud praying, his hand caressing hers, hoping that God had given Young a different kind of treasure than he'd sacrificed his earthly life for.

Sara sighed, shoving back the hair that had escaped its ponytail. "I can hardly read this list. Tom has terrible handwriting."

He tried for levity. "I'll alert his elementary school teacher to rescind his diploma."

"I'm too tired and scared to find that funny."

She looked exhausted, dark circles showing under her eyes, her shoulders slumped. It was time to deploy his surprise, he decided. Reaching into his pocket, he pulled out the squashed candy bar. "I saved this for you."

He thought he actually saw tears of happiness glimmering against her lashes and felt like laughing with joy.

She looked at the dismal offering as if it was a turkey dinner with all the trimmings.

"Chocolate?" she gasped. "You didn't eat yours?"

"Nah. Figured you might want it later. I don't like chocolate, anyway. You know that."

She stared at him as though he were an alien amoeba from some faraway galaxy. "I still cannot comprehend anyone not liking chocolate."

"You never complained while we were dating. You always ate the brownies Mrs. Grossman gave me." He'd enjoyed giving them to her, watching her make a big show of packing them away to share with her family and then seeing her eating them all by herself when she thought no one was looking.

He watched her bite into the banged-up chocolate, eyes closing in pleasure, a soft moan welling up from deep in her throat. A cheap candy bar brought more happiness than anything else he could have rustled up. He was thrilled that he'd been able to give her respite, even if it was only for a moment, a second or two of distraction from the deadline looming over their heads.

She finished the chocolate down to the last bit, searching the wrapper for any tiny remnant she might have missed before she let out a gusty sigh. "That was wonderful. Thank you."

He chuckled. If they ever got out of the current mess, he resolved to send her a candy bar every month, no matter where in the world they both landed. It was selfish, probably, to want her to think about him, at least for a moment or two. Seemed only fair, since he knew he would never stop thinking about her.

It was fully dark outside now, sometime between nine and eleven, he estimated. He didn't know if Beretta would hold tightly to his hour deadline, but they had to come up with something to placate him and buy more time. He read over her shoulder.

"Lookout, vacation, spotting," he said again. "It sounds meaningless, but there's got to be a reason he listed them, unless it was just plain delirium."

Licking her lips, she read the paper again before she threw it down and pressed her hands to her eyes. "I can't. I'm empty. This isn't going to work, is it? Beretta is going to kill us. We might as well just let him get it over with." Now the tears really were trickling down her face. She was as strong as any woman he'd ever met, but chocolate or no chocolate, she was coming to the end of her reserves.

He knelt in front of her and gathered her close. He exalted in the warmth of her skin against his, the strength in her slender body that had labored so hard to keep both him and Del Young alive. Now it was his turn to be strong for the both of them.

"We are going to get out of this, Sarah."

"I don't see how. I can't solve the case."

"Didn't you say to me once that faith was not seeing, but believing anyway?"

She sniffed, the tears continuing to trickle down her cheeks. He used his sleeve to dab them away. "Hey," he said, propping up her chin to meet his gaze. "We're not defeated yet."

"I'm sorry Marco told you to look out for me," she said, shaking her head, "that you got into this mess because of me."

"I'm not sorry," he said.

She drew back and stared at him, swiping at her nose with the sleeve of her baggy coveralls. He'd seen Sarah decked out for prom and dressed to the nines for a wedding, but he'd never thought her so lovely as he did then, swathed in dirty blue coveralls, her face exquisitely tender and grave. He was privileged to be the one standing with her through this horror, honored to be the one who was chosen to spend what might be their last moments together. *Thank You, God. Thank You for letting it be me.*

She was staring at him, head cocked to the side, fervent eyes searching his face. "Surely you would not choose to be in this situation with me, the girl who broke your heart."

He didn't answer at first, just cupped a hand to her cheek and pressed his lips to her temple. "Being with you has allowed me to resolve a few things."

"What things?"

"Plans for the future, for one." His senses were dizzied by her proximity, and for a moment, he wanted to believe that they were still in love. He longed for it with an intensity he hadn't realized he possessed, but his heart, even in its battered condition, would not accept the untruth. Sarah did not love him. They were two people who shared a history, thrown together in desperate circumstances, struggling to survive. He read it in her stiffening posture, the way she subtly drew away from him.

Though he wanted to keep her close, he let go and she sat back, breaking his hold on her.

"I've resolved a few things, too," she said. "I really am going to take a break from nursing if we live through this. I was doubting my decision, but I think it's the right one. I feel like God's telling me to start a new chapter in my life. My father's gone, I've been drifting around, afraid to begin again without him, but now I know it's time."

A new chapter. New life. He found it hard to swallow. *High school's over, Jett.* His hard-earned wisdom had come too late. He was a part of the past she was trying to put behind her. He cleared his throat. "When we get out of this, I'm going to make a few changes, too."

"So sure we'll make it through?" she said shakily.

He nodded. "One hundred percent."

"What will you do?"

"We don't need to go into it now."

"Please," she begged. "Talk to me about something besides clues and paintings and death waiting on the other side of that door. Tell me about the future, your future."

He gave voice to the plan that had sparked in his mind those long hours lying on his cot. "Gonna go back to college. Get a degree in business and open my own dive company."

She smiled. "Perfect. A life on the water just like you always wanted." She paused. "Where will you set up shop?"

"Not sure. Got any suggestions?"

"Maybe near Laguna Beach, where your mom is."

"Yeah," he said, something heavy settling in his heart. "That might be good." He realized he'd desperately wanted her to suggest he stay in Coronado, where she lived. Stupid of him. He'd resolved the past, so he could move on to another future. One without her. It was what she wanted. What was right for them both, and he'd expected nothing else. He wondered why it felt like there was an anchor inside him. Had he thought for a fleeting moment that she still wanted him? That there might be some ember left between them that could be fanned to life? *No way, Jett. You threw away a future with Sarah long ago. Any feelings you might have imagined between you are due to this ridiculous scenario you're ensnared in.*

"So you'll be a detective, and I'll be a dive master. Funny how life turns out, isn't it?"

"Yes, funny." She looked as though she wanted to say something else, but instead she picked up the paper. "We have to get back to business."

Yes, he thought, *the business of survival*. He rubbed a hand over his eyes and stood, pacing again, ignoring the various aches and pains that flared up in his body. "Del Young must have another place farther south, because he spent plenty of time with Mary Ellsworth. I'm going to guess he's stashed the painting somewhere nearby."

She nodded. "Makes sense, since it would be risky to fly or drive it anywhere until he was ready to hand it over to Beretta. Lookout, vacation, spotting. What do they have in common?"

"Lookout and spotting." Jett puzzled it over. "Vacation? Fire lookouts? Whale spotting?" He shook his head. "You could go on a whale spotting vacation, I suppose. I have no idea what that would have to do with hiding *The Red Lady*."

Sarah's frame went rigid. She bolted to her feet.

"What?"

"I just thought of something."

"Well, don't keep me in suspense. Let's have it."

"Jett," she said, eyes sparkling with wonder. With the pencil she'd stuck behind her ear, she crossed something out and wrote on the paper. "What if he didn't say vacation? What if he said 'station'?"

"Lookout, spotting, station." Jett's pulse flickered. "A spotting station, as in a World War II spotting station? The kind that looks out across the Pacific Ocean."

"Yes, there were many sprinkled along the California coast."

"Uh-huh. I read all about them when I was a kid. The men who manned the stations would use azimuth scopes to take the bearings of enemy ships. They were experts on identifying the ships' silhouettes."

"You know," she said slowly, "there's a spotting station in Santa Barbara. It's been boarded up to keep out the vandals and teens looking to party there. My father took us once years ago, before they closed off the place. I remember it was set on a bluff away from everything, no houses or buildings nearby."

"A World War II spotting station," he repeated. "The perfect place to hide something."

"And someone? Could Mary be there, too? Camped out and waiting for him to return?"

"Unlikely, after all this time, but they may have arranged to meet there when he messaged her the deal with Beretta was done." Jett heard footsteps in the hallway. "Are you sure about this, Sarah?"

He heard her swallow. "No, I'm not, but I don't think there's time for a plan B."

"Then we go with plan A," he said, taking her hand and squaring his shoulders. "Sarah Gal, it's time to solve this mystery one way or another."

She clung to his hand. "I'm scared, Jett."

"We'll finish this together," he said, kissing her temple.

She pressed her trembling lips together and gave him one brave nod.

Miguel opened the door for Beretta. He stepped inside. The gun was not in his hand, but Jett saw it holstered at the belt.

"So what is it to be?" Beretta said. "You solved the case or you are to be shot?"

Jett smiled. "She solved the case. She knows where *The Red Lady* is."

"But I want to confirm it with Marco and Candace, when they call."

He looked at an expensive gold watch on his wrist. "And with five minutes to spare? Let us not wait any longer. Tell me what you have discovered."

"I might be wrong. My family can confirm and—"

"They're lying," Miguel growled. "You see?"

Beretta silenced him with an upheld palm. "Tell me. Now."

"How do we know you aren't going to kill us as soon as we tell you?" Sarah said.

"You don't," he said, "but my painting is worth thirty million dollars and change. We did not capture Tom and Ellsworth, so if they have figured out the clues, they might be headed for the same location. You will lead me to it first, and then, perhaps if I am feeling gracious, I will let you go."

"And if we don't?" Jett said.

"You will." Beretta's smile was wolfish. "Because you do not wish to see this lady grievously hurt. I am correct, no? I saw the rage in your eyes when I shot at her earlier. I know that you will do anything to keep me from putting a bullet into her for real, won't you?"

Jett fumed, the blood in his body turning to lava. If she wasn't standing next to him, he'd have thrown himself at Beretta, gun or no gun. He'd taken on plenty of tough guys in his day, and Beretta was no better than your average street-corner thug.

Miguel stood nearby, daring him to act.

"All right," Jett said, tamping down on his anger with an extreme effort. "We'll take you there, tomorrow. It's on the mainland, but the channel is treacherous at night."

"Not to worry," Beretta said. "We have a boat and

we are experienced in navigating difficult waters, so to speak."

"We should wait until morning," Jett said firmly.

Beretta turned to stare at Jett. It was not the look of a man who was accustomed to waiting.

And if they delivered on finding the painting, would Beretta actually let them go?

He did not have the look of a man who was accustomed to mercy, either.

As they were escorted from the room at gunpoint, Miguel's burner phone began to ring. "Let me speak to them, just to be sure."

With a snicker of laughter, Miguel tossed the phone on the bed where Del Young's body lay and closed the door behind them, the phone ringing in the empty room.

TWENTY

Alex was sent to prepare Beretta's boat for departure. Jett felt as if time was slowing down, the minutes dragging by in slow motion. He knew Marco and Sarah's sisters would find them soon. The police would have to come also, when the downed chopper was discovered or the pilot's family filed a missing persons report. It was a matter of time, a cat and mouse game to see if they could survive until help arrived.

His idea of deciphering Young's note had bought them some precious minutes, and what's more it would get them off the island, which might open up another avenue of escape. Jett eyed the list Sarah still clutched in her hand. If Miguel would just divert his attention for a minute, one of them could write a note with their intended location and a message incriminating Antonio Beretta and his men. It wasn't much of a bread-crumb trail, but it was something.

But Miguel watched them closely, even as Beretta whispered something into his ear.

"You can't just leave Mr. Young here," Sarah was saying as he led them down the stairs.

Miguel snorted. "He won't care one way or another."

She gaped and shook her head as if she could not think

of anything further to convince these men to behave like civilized beings.

When they reached the bottom floor, Miguel motioned for them to follow, his pistol in his hand.

They were marched down the hallway. Jett was surprised and alarmed when they stopped at the entrance to Ellsworth's art gallery. Beretta stepped inside and motioned for them to join him in the softly lit room.

They were stopping to appreciate Ellsworth's collection? Something felt very wrong. Jett stayed close to Sarah, virtually shoulder to shoulder with her as they shuffled across the plush carpeted floor.

The gallery was pristine except for the pile of papers dumped in the middle of the room. Jett's nerves prickled. Beretta walked close to several of the pictures, his nose inches from the canvas.

"Do you have an appreciation for art?" Beretta asked. When they remained silent, he continued. "You think of me as a thug, a lowlife, yet I know more about art than either one of you."

"Knowledge isn't what you're lacking," Jett said.

"Ellsworth has some fine pieces," Beretta continued as if he hadn't heard, absorbed in his study of the artwork, "but none as excellent as mine." He neared a small abstract of waves thundering against a rocky coastline. "Except for this one. It is a Joseph Turner, an artist I do not possess. He was an English landscape painter. His mother was mad, apparently." He lifted it from the wall, studying the rich wood frame and the bold colors. "Genius. Truly a master."

"So you're going to steal it?" Jett said. "Just like Ellsworth arranged to steal *The Red Lady*?"

"Exactly. I will take what is his and punish him tenfold." Gazing at the painting, he moved it so the light would play on different parts of the work. "I will give this to my wife for her birthday."

"Nothing says love like giving your sweetheart a stolen painting," Jett muttered. He saw Sarah smile, a hard-won prize.

Beretta laughed. "And nothing says revenge quite like this." He pulled a lighter from his pocket and flicked it to life. The little orange flame reflected in Beretta's dark eyes.

Jett's breath hitched as he understood. "Don't. These pieces are one of a kind. They were meant to be seen."

"And I have seen them. Ellsworth, however, should he live to return to his island, will never enjoy them again."

"No," Sarah cried. "You can't destroy them."

"Watch me," he said as he touched the lighter to the piece of paper atop the pile. It caught, a little flame flaring up and spreading to engulf the paper next to it. The glint of the orange fire leaped up and painted his skin in garish light.

Madness, Jett thought. *This is what madness looks like, or maybe addiction.* He thought of his father, so hopelessly addicted to alcohol that he could not be the man, the husband, the father he was meant to be. Jett was now standing face-to-face with another man who was so addicted to power that he would destroy wondrous treasures simply because he could not possess them. Ellsworth, abducting people and ready to torture others over *The Red Lady*. Beretta, crazy with rage at being bested. How could Jett have ever figured he could make it through this broken world without God?

Thanks, Lord, he said silently. *However it goes, thanks for helping me see the truth.*

The flames were devouring the papers and reaching outward to the carpet now, but Beretta did not seem inclined to leave. He watched, transfixed, as the fire licked toward the walls, creeping inch by inch upward, feeding like hungry serpents.

Some of the frames caught. With a crackle and pop, the fire ate away the nearest portrait of a young boy standing on the bow of a ship. His golden hair blistered, charred and peeled away in sooty flakes before the twisted mass fell to the floor and became part of the bonfire. Sarah turned and pressed her face to Jett's chest.

He stroked her hair, turning his own gaze away from the sickening destruction, focusing on the treasure he held in his arms as the others incinerated around them, the fire fueled by anger and avarice.

"Mr. Beretta?" Miguel said, shifting uneasily as smoke began to fill the room. "The fire will attract attention."

"I hope so," Beretta said. "I hope Ellsworth can see it from wherever he is holed up."

"We should leave," Miguel insisted.

Beretta seemed to snap back to reality. "I will package my new Turner, and we will go get *The Red Lady.*"

Sarah tensed in his arms.

Such a simple plan, Jett thought. Would there really be a priceless painting hidden in the abandoned spotting station? Or were they wrong, hopelessly wrong?

More importantly, he thought, as he led Sarah out of the room, would there be an opportunity for them to escape once they were off the wretched island? Resolved to stay alert for the slightest opportunity, Jett kept his arm around Sarah as they were marched toward the dock.

Sarah's coveralls were damp with fog and the spray of the waves as Miguel piloted the boat to the Santa Barbara coast. The cold stiffened her body and brought every scratch and contusion groaning to life. She wished they had been able to keep the yellow rain slickers, because she was now doused to the skin. They tied the boat up, and Beretta sent Miguel to obtain a vehicle. They were kept in the front, while Beretta held a gun on them from the back, smoking his cigarettes until Sarah wanted to retch from the acrid smell.

Miguel returned a half hour later with a green SUV. Sarah only hoped he had not killed someone when he'd stolen it.

They got in, and Jett was forced to drive with Miguel in the passenger seat and Sarah in the back with Beretta. They drove through the empty streets of Santa Barbara. She directed Miguel toward a steep road at the edge of town that led up the cliffs, praying her long-ago memory would not fail her. The night was crisp and clear, the sky washed with a faint veil of clouds.

"Where?" Miguel demanded when the road forked off in two different directions.

"To the right," Sarah said, more confidently than she felt.

He complied, guiding the vehicle up the steep trail.

Sarah had a vivid memory of hiking up to the spotting station with her father. She couldn't have been more than thirteen, sullen over having to miss a day with her friends, grumbling over the exertion of climbing the steep hill on foot with their picnic lunches stowed in their backpacks. But the sweeping panorama wasn't what she remembered from that day. They'd encountered an old man in stained clothes and dirty shirtsleeves there in the spotting station. Sarah had been afraid of the man with the wrinkled face and the missing front tooth, but her father had promptly sat down next to the man and invited him to share their picnic lunch, handing over half of his own sandwich to the stranger. By the time the meal was done, Bruce Gallagher found out the homeless man was a Vietnam vet with a drinking problem and nowhere to go. Her father passed along the name and address of their church, the local homeless shelter and the offer of a ride if it was desired. Bruce also left the man his jacket and another sandwich when they departed.

Sarah remembered looking at her father differently after that day. Before then, Bruce Gallagher was her father. After that, he was a man who would literally give someone the shirt off his back. That day, a moment at the spotting station had changed her life. Now, it seemed, her life would once again be forever changed by what happened at the old stone bunker.

Jett stopped the car when he reached a barrier in the road. A metal railing was drawn across to prevent vehicles from passing, but Miguel took care of the padlock by shooting it. The rail surrendered with a shrill squeal as he shoved it out of the way.

Returning to the car, Miguel rolled down the window. Cold air blasted her face, leaving it stiff with the chill. Outside the wind scoured the rocks, which shone bald and blunt in the moonlight. The night was silent save for the sound of the waves, the moaning of the breeze and the pounding of her own heart in her ears.

She thought about Mary Ellsworth. Had Young really abducted her as Ellsworth claimed? If so, and he'd imprisoned her in the spotting station, she would surely no longer be alive after so many days had passed. Or was she an accomplice, in love with Young and trying to help him fence the painting he'd stolen from her father? Had she given up waiting for him to return and struck out on her own? They might have the answer in minutes. Her skin prickled in anxiety as they approached.

Jett appeared relaxed in the driver's seat, but she knew

by the muscle jumping in his jaw that he was thinking through all the possible escape scenarios. With both Miguel and Beretta armed and ready to kill them as soon as they found—or did not find—the painting, she did not see that there were any scenarios at all.

As he stared out the front window, she looked again at his strong profile, recalling her utter despair when she'd cradled him in her arms, thinking he'd drowned. God helped her to drag Jett from that ocean, she told herself sternly. It was not over until He willed it to be.

Still, she felt a sharp pang of guilt. Jett was here because of her. He'd let her down in a big way in high school, and in some ways, she'd let him down also. Now here they were, at the bitter end of the horrific adventure. She realized there was no one she would rather have at her side. Scarred, failed, saved and still strong. Jett had never left her heart for a moment and he never would. If only she could tell him, thank him one more time, express to him that she knew he would make an amazing success of his dive business, of his life, of a marriage.

Her heart throbbed as she thought of it. What they could have had, how they'd been so foolish.

The SUV stopped at an outcropping of rock. About twenty yards distant, the spotting station loomed like an enormous concrete mushroom at the edge of the cliff. It had only a boarded-up door on one side and a narrow horizontal slit traversing the cement on the other, where the spotters would keep their lookout to warn of enemy ships approaching. They got out of the car and Miguel shoved Jett toward the boarded-up door.

"Open it."

Jett gripped one of the weather-roughened boards and pulled. It came away easily in his grasp. "It's been opened recently," he called.

Sarah could hardly keep still. Maybe Young had been there, and Mary, too. Jett removed the rest of the boards and yanked open the door. A waft of cold, dank air bathed her face. She could make out a set of concrete steps, cracked and damp.

Miguel ordered them up. Jett went first, his head barely clearing the low overhead cement. Sarah tucked her fingers into his belt loop and followed. They were not offered flashlights, so they picked their way along one slippery step at a time. The stairs opened into a large oval room. Dry pine needles crunched under her feet, and the chill seeped up through the thin soles of her shoes.

"Now," Beretta said. "Let's see if you were right about my *Lady*."

Sarah held her breath as Beretta and Miguel turned on their flashlights.

For a moment the illumination dazzled her eyes. As she adjusted, Miguel pushed them farther into the circular space.

"There's nothing here," Jett said at last.

Sarah felt her heart plummet as the flashlight beams picked out only the blanket of pine needles. No boxes or wrapped package. No sign that Mary or Young had ever been there.

"It seems you were wrong," Beretta said, through clenched teeth. He drew his pistol and aimed.

"No," Sarah cried, just as two figures emerged at the top of the stairs, one firing a shot that exploded through the chamber.

Jett flung himself on top of Sarah and they rolled toward a thick pile of needles accumulated on the damp floor. At first in the gloom and the confusion, he did not recognize the two people silhouetted by lantern light.

"Everyone stay still," Tom commanded, the gun in his right hand. In his left, he held a powerful lantern.

Mr. Ellsworth's face was like something from a zombie movie. His cheekbone was bruised, lip split, probably at the hands of Miguel or Beretta before his escape. Holding a smaller lantern, he moved by Tom as if in a trance. "Where is she?" he said, head swiveling.

Beretta was on the floor, nursing the wound in his shin where Tom had shot him. "Drop it," Tom said to Miguel, and he reluctantly lowered his gun to the floor.

Ellsworth caught sight of Jett and Sarah. He fell to his knees. "Mary," he gasped.

Sarah looked at him, breathing hard. Jett stayed in front of Sarah, but she peeked over his outstretched arm. "Mary isn't here, Mr. Ellsworth. I'm Sarah Gallagher."

"Where's Mary? And *The Red Lady*?" Ellsworth asked.

Jett thought Tom looked slightly sick.

"You followed my tracking bracelet, Tom?"

Tom nodded, eyes still on Ellsworth.

"Is the painting here?" Ellsworth said.

"No," Miguel snapped. "There's nothing here."

Jett gaped as Sarah stood up. "Yes, there is," she said. From underneath the debris she removed a rectangular, plastic-wrapped package. As she removed the tape, they watched openmouthed. Sarah revealed the portrait. In the lamplight, the face of the *The Red Lady* seemed almost real, as if she'd been expecting them to arrive. Her painted eyes glimmered with animation, the curve of her neck elegant in the gloom.

"Ah," Ellsworth said. "There she is."

"Get away from that." Beretta stood on one leg and started toward Ellsworth. "It's mine."

Tom stopped him. "Not anymore. We're walking out of here, right now."

"Not without my Mary," Ellsworth said.

"She's not here." Tom's face was pained. "She's not here, okay? Can't you see that?"

Miguel cocked his head. "I hear sirens. We need to go, Mr. Beretta."

Jett's heart leaped. The cops. If they could just survive a few moments longer.

"Not until I get my painting," Beretta roared, lunging for Sarah.

Jett intercepted him with a football tackle to his midriff. The breath whooshed out of Beretta and they crashed to the floor. Beretta lashed out an elbow, knocking Jett back and reaching for the gun at his belt, but Jett hung onto his wrist, clinging with every last ounce of strength.

Miguel lurched toward them, but Tom fired a shot that caught Miguel in the arm. He clapped a hand to his bicep, groaning in pain.

Jett finally got the drop on Beretta and twisted his arms behind his back. Miguel looked at his fallen boss, and after a moment of thought, sprinted toward the door and disappeared down the stairs.

Mr. Ellsworth stood shakily and approached Sarah, arms out for the painting. "Mary left it for me."

"Stop saying that," Tom shouted. "You know she didn't. Mary's not here, and she never was."

Jett kept his hold on Beretta. "Where is Mary Ellsworth, Tom?" Jett said. "You know, don't you?"

His mouth twitched, but he did not answer.

"Hand me the painting," Tom said, pointing the gun at Sarah.

"Give it to him, Sarah," Jett said.

"No," Beretta shouted, writhing in Jett's grip. It was all he could do to hold on to the man. If he let Beretta go, he'd be on Sarah in a second. If he didn't, Tom might get tired of waiting and shoot her. Sweat beaded his forehead as he tried to figure out which was the best choice to keep her safe.

"What happened to Mary?" Jett called to Mr. Ellsworth.

Ellsworth looked at him as if they'd never met. "It wasn't supposed to be her."

"Shut up," Tom yelled.

"It was Young. He cheated me, lied about not being able to steal *The Red Lady*, and then he kept my money, so we arranged an accident." Ellsworth's voice sounded dreamy. "To hurt Mr. Young, to punish him, but not to kill him."

Jett and Sarah locked eyes. Something bad was coming. Something worse than art theft and abduction and greed. "Mr. Ellsworth," he said again slowly. "Where is Mary?"

There was a sound of boots pounding up the steps, and Marco barreled through with Candace right behind him.

"She's dead," Candace said from behind Marco's shoulder. He stood in front, Ka-Bar in his fist. Jett had never been so happy to see his ornery mentor.

"Mary Ellsworth died three months ago in a Jet Ski accident." Candace's eyes flew to her sister. "Sarah," she breathed. "Oh, Sarah."

Sarah stood with the painting in her hands. "I'm okay," she said, tears glinting in the lantern light.

"We figured it had to be the spotting station," Candace said in a whisper.

"And you were right," Sarah said.

Marco edged in, trying to move closer to Tom.

"Stay there," Tom said. "Or I'll shoot her."

Marco stopped but he did not lower the knife. "That'd be a bad idea," he growled softly.

"Mary's dead," Ellsworth said. "Mary's dead and it was supposed to be Del Young. I had Tom sabotage his Jet Ski motor, but Mary took it out instead. She's dead," he said again, saying the words slowly and carefully. "Mary is dead."

"Yes, you stupid fool," Tom yelled. "Now all that's left is this painting. I'm not going to follow orders anymore. I loved her, too. How do you think it feels to know I helped kill her? Did you think you were the only one who felt anything for Mary?"

Dead at the hands of her own father, Jett thought, worst of all. No wonder Ellsworth had gone mad, dreaming up some crazy scenario in which Mary was alive and hiding out with his coveted painting.

Tom moved closer to Sarah. "Hand me the painting, and then I'm leaving. You can do what you want with him," he said, jerking his head toward his boss.

Ellsworth was rocking back and forth, moaning. He stretched out his hands toward the painting. "Give her to me," he rasped.

Tom fired off a round that ricocheted off the concrete, sending sparks and chips of cement flying before it embedded itself in the far wall.

Sarah lifted the painting, and before Tom could grab it, she shoved it almost all the way through the narrow slot in the cement. It teetered on the edge.

"No," Tom and Beretta shouted at once.

"If you don't put the gun down, I'm going to drop her through," Sarah said. "She'll fall fifty feet and hit the rocks below."

Jett stared at Sarah. He knew she was terrified, her body trembling, yet in her face was such courage he knew that she had the strength to overcome anything—a lost father, a new career, their own dark past. He resolved at that moment if there was any breath in his body, he was going to spend his life standing by her side. She was too magnificent, too filled with spirit and heart for him to ever live without.

If only he could convince her.

If only they could get out of the situation alive.

Tom went rigid with anger. "That's a thirty-million-dollar painting."

Sarah shrugged a shoulder. "So sue me."

Jett wanted to kiss her. But then Tom's finger closed on the trigger and there was no longer time to wait. He sprang off Beretta and dived at Tom. The gun fired and Jett felt a line of heat crease his temple. Stars swirled in his field of vision, but he got his weight onto Tom's gun arm and bore down with everything he had.

Marco rushed for his other arm, and between them, Tom relinquished his grip on his gun. It skidded from his fingers.

Out of the corner of his eye, Jett saw Beretta surge to his feet. Sarah hurled the painting at him Frisbee style. He was so startled that he grabbed for it with both hands. At the same moment, Candace cracked him over the head with her binoculars. It did not knock him out, but it stunned him for a precious moment and he sank to his knees, the painting settling onto his lap.

Jett looked to Marco, not yet letting go of Tom. "You got this?"

"You have to ask?" Marco said.

Jett released Tom to Marco and removed *The Red Lady* from Beretta's lap and twisted his arms behind his back. Marco pulled two zip ties from the cargo pocket on his pants and tossed one to Jett, who tied Beretta while Marco did the same with Tom.

They marched the two men halfway down the stairs,

where two uniformed officers were just charging up, guns drawn.

"We got the other guy on his way down the road," the taller cop said.

"Well, here's another couple of clients for you." Jett was only too happy to hand Tom and Beretta into their custody. "One more upstairs."

They returned to find Mr. Ellsworth stroking *The Red Lady*'s frame, crooning to her as if the canvas and paint were his lost daughter. The sight sickened Jett.

Candace still had one eye on Ellsworth and her binoculars gripped in her hands, as if she expected she might have to conk him over the head at any moment.

"I got him now," Marco said, helping Ellsworth to his feet and ushering him into the custody of another newly arrived cop. "You can put the binoculars away."

Candace dropped her arms and wrapped her sister in a smothering hug.

"I was so afraid, Sarah," Candace cried. "I felt so helpless knowing you were in danger." And then she dissolved into tears.

Sarah was swallowed up in her sister's embrace. "I knew you were looking for us, all of you. I love you, big sister."

"Love you, too, little sister," Candace choked out.

Jett backed up a few steps, letting the women sob together. The sibling bond was something he'd never experienced, but it was clear that Candace was exactly what Sarah needed.

Marco joined him. "All right, Jett?"

"Yes, sir, but it was dicey there at the end. What took you so long?"

"Didn't want to interrupt your island vacation."

He laughed. "Considerate."

Marco pointed to Jett's head wound. "Forgot to duck?"

"Yes, sir."

"Serious?"

"No, just a scratch."

"Okay then."

Candace pulled Sarah to arm's length and stroked her face, speaking low and soft to her sister, sentiments Jett could not hear and probably would not understand anyway. He had his own sentiments to unburden.

Later. The events of the past few hours unrolled in his mind like a long stretch of road, culminating in the life-and-death struggle in the old spotting station. He could not quite get his mind to accept all the things that had happened. One ridiculous detail rose to the top.

"Marco?"

"Yeah?"

"Did Candace really just take down drug kingpin Antonio Beretta with a pair of binoculars?"

Marco grinned. "Affirmative. Nice piece of work."

"You teach her that from your navy SEAL arsenal?"

"Nope. Came up with that one herself. Like Sarah threatening to drop *The Red Lady*."

They both continued to gaze at Candace and Sarah.

"Girls," Jett said. "They're unpredictable."

"You got that right," Marco said with a chuckle.

Sarah disentangled herself from her sister and made her way to Jett.

He took her hands.

"Are you hurt?" she said, voice unsteady.

"No. You?"

She shook her head. "I can't believe it's over."

"Believe it." He stroked her fingers. "We're safe."

She sucked in a breath and the tears began to trickle

down her face. He folded her in his arms and kissed the top of her head.

Thank You, God, was all he could manage as he tried not to squeeze her too tightly to his chest. They had not been defeated, not by the ocean, not by Beretta or Ellsworth and not by their own past mistakes. He felt nothing but pure joy that Sarah, the most precious treasure in his life, was alive and safe.

Three days later, Jett attended the art auction for one reason only—because Sarah, along with the Gallagher clan, was going to be there. He'd spent the last seventy-two hours going over the details of their ordeal with police and enduring medical checkups. Sarah had been undergoing the same and he had not had a private moment with her since they returned to Coronado. The object of Beretta and Ellsworth's obsession, *The Red Lady*, had been seized by the Mexican government after Beretta was jailed, and by some confusing twists and turns it was now up for auction again. He hoped the new owner would be a more savory character.

Marco met him before he entered, looking conspicuous in jeans and a T-shirt. The auction required a jacket and tie and Marco was philosophically opposed to both, so he waited outside, unwilling to leave them unescorted until he was sure Beretta's people planned no retaliation. The key players were in jail in Mexico, but a powerful man like Beretta would not stay there for long, nor would he forget who put him there.

Marco considered the question Jett had just posed to him. "Sarah is the baby, you know. We're protective of her."

"Yes, sir, I know."

"And I still think you should have bested Beretta's men at the clinic. I mean, it was only three of them."

"Yes, sir."

"You need more boxing lessons?"

"Apparently."

Marco nodded, falling into a silence that lasted nearly two minutes. Jett knew better than to interrupt, so he shoved his hands in the pockets of his slacks and waited.

"So you really think you're good enough for her?" Marco demanded, arms folded across his burly chest.

"No, sir."

"That's right. You're not. So whatcha gonna do about that?"

"Going to spend the rest of my life trying to be worthy of her love, if she'll have me."

Marco nodded. "Affirmative, and if you ever mess up and hurt her…"

"I'm going to answer to you."

"That's another affirmative."

They lingered in silence for another few minutes until Marco straightened. "All right then. As long as we've got that straight."

Marco shook Jett's hand in a bear grip, and though he never cracked a smile, Jett thought his mentor's mouth quirked in pleasure—at least he imagined it had. The big man turned to leave.

"Marco…" Jett looked his father figure in the eye. He wanted to thank the man who had changed the trajectory of his life, who gave him a chance to become the person he wanted to be, the one who had taken a risk on a skinny, loudmouthed kid with no hope and no help. He wanted to say so many things, but he found himself unable to utter a word through the sudden clog in his throat.

Marco stared back at Jett for a moment and nodded,

hopefully hearing all that Jett could not say. He gave one final shake and clasped Jett in a quick, bone-crushing hug. "Get on with it."

And then he walked away.

Jett wandered into the auction house, settling into the back row. He admired *The Red Lady*, on display in all her glory on a sturdy stand. She looked every inch the regal lady in that gallery setting, and he found it hard to believe that Sarah had almost pitched her out of the spotting station onto the rocks. That made him smile.

He settled in, enjoying the comfort of the soft chair, the sensation of clean clothes, a full stomach and no more tracking bracelet around his ankle. And then it began—a genteel dogfight to see who would become the next owner of *The Red Lady*. He only hoped it would be a more worthy individual than the two who'd tried so desperately to acquire her before.

When the event was done, one fortunate businessman from Japan was the proud owner of the *The Red Lady* for a cool thirty million dollars and change. He beamed and accepted congratulations for his new acquisition. The painting would probably go immediately into a climate-controlled gallery, sealed away from all but a few select visitors. Those folks would never know how the painting had been caught up in a deadly adventure involving two countries, two vicious adversaries and the loss of several lives. As the gallery began to clear, he made his way out.

He caught up with Sarah in the lush courtyard. She was surrounded by her mother and sisters, who bustled her along like a duckling. In the distance, Marco waited, leaning on the hood of his truck, ever vigilant.

Seeing Sarah there, ringed by her family, almost made him lose his nerve.

They remember me as a loser, the high school drop-out, a troublemaker.

His palms went cold, but he forced his feet forward. Finally, JeanBeth Gallagher turned around and spotted him. He wasn't sure whether to wave or offer a handshake to Sarah's mother. While he puzzled it over, she closed the gap between them.

"Dominic," she said, throwing her arms around him and kissing his cheek. "How can we thank you enough for what you did for Sarah?"

"She did a lot for me, too, Mrs. Gallagher," he said.

Donna, Candace and Angela Gallagher added their hugs and kisses while Sarah stood by, her cheeks pink. When they were done, JeanBeth took his hand and smiled. "I've heard the condensed version of what happened on that island, but I'd love to know the rest of the details. It's pot roast night, and you're invited. We're celebrating. You and Sarah are safely returned, and even *The Red Lady* survived the ordeal."

"Oh, well, I'm not sure…"

"Six thirty." Mrs. Gallagher tugged playfully at his lapel. "Don't be late or you have to do all the dishes by yourself."

Angela laughed. "That's really more of a command than an invitation, I hope you realize."

"Yep," Donna said. "Don't make us track you down. We're detectives, you know. We can do that."

He almost felt like part of the family for a moment. "Thank you."

"No," JeanBeth said, face suddenly serious. "Thank you." She kissed him one more time and then the Gallaghers continued on up the walkway. Sarah started to follow.

"Sarah, can I talk to you?"

She turned those green-gold eyes on him, accentuated by the pale green silk of her dress, and his breath hitched. A strand of pearls decorated her throat, and her hair was gathered softly at the base of her neck. More beautiful than *The Red Lady*, or any other priceless work of art. He felt himself go hot, then cold.

"Just for a minute," he mumbled.

"Um, okay," she said. She took his offered arm and walked with him down the path toward the shade of some flowering shrubs.

"Don't feel pressured into pot roast night, by the way," she said, giving his arm a playful squeeze. "My mother is forceful."

"Runs in the family."

She laughed. "Dad used to say she was an undercover general." Her expression grew serious. "I know my mom and sisters said it, but I'm not sure I have, not enough anyway. Thank you, Jett." She tipped her head up to look in his eyes, sun shining on the glossy satin of her skin. "I would not be alive if it wasn't for you."

"I could say the same. I'd be floating somewhere in the ocean without your help. Food for the fishes."

She blushed a deeper shade of petal pink. "Well, anyway, we both came out of it alive, by the grace of God. Are you okay?" Reaching up, she touched his bandaged temple very gently with her forefinger, sending tingles along his face and neck. "No lasting damage?"

"Nah, just maybe a scar to enhance my good looks. It will give me something to tell my grandkids about someday."

Another brilliant smile from her circled right to the core of him. He wanted so desperately to speak, but the words froze inside him and the silence lengthened.

"Well, I…guess I'd better go," Sarah said wistfully.

"My family are keeping me on a tight leash since I got back."

"Wait. I've gotta tell you something," he blurted.

"What?"

"I did it. I mean, I enrolled in night classes and put a deposit down on a space for my dive company office."

"That's awesome."

"Here in Coronado."

She blinked. "Really? Right here?"

His heart hammered in his throat. "Yeah. Want to stay close to Marco." Had he really said that?

She offered a wry smile. "Marco does need a man around. All these women drive him to the point of distraction. I think that's why he spends so much time at the gym."

"And you. I mean, I wanted to be close to you."

Her mouth formed a little O of surprise. "Me?"

"Yes." His tongue simply wouldn't cooperate with her staring at him, those lush lips parted in surprise, the flicker of her lashes, the way her hair smelled like flowers. Everything he wanted to say turned into a jumble in his mouth when he looked into her eyes.

"Just a minute."

He turned her around so she was facing away from him. "Now I'm gonna say it without getting mixed up." He sucked in a deep breath and blurted, "I love you," to the back of her head.

He saw her shoulders lift in surprise.

"I've always loved you," he hurried on. "When my life was in tatters and I hated myself, you were the one thing that shone bright, like some sort of star or something. And on the island, when you gave everything you had to keep me alive, I saw it again. I think maybe it's your soul that peeks out from inside." He was babbling, words flying out like wild ocean spray, nerves firing wildly as he tried to read her body language.

Her head was bowed now, and his gut twisted, wondering if she was ready to turn around and send him packing.

Go for broke, Jett. Initial success or total failure. He reached for her, resting his fingers on the delicate blades of her shoulders. Could he feel her trembling, or was it his own nerves getting in the way?

"On the island, when I almost drowned, God reminded me that I have a soul, too. It's kinda bashed up and torn, I think, but He let my soul shine through the mess I've made of things. Sort of gave me a second chance, I guess and I'm not gonna waste it." He sucked in a strengthening breath. "I understand if you don't feel the same way about me, Sarah, but I had to say it. I had to tell you, because second chances don't come around very often."

She'd still not made a sound. He swallowed hard, willing her to feel the love through his fingertips.

"If your father was around, I would have asked him first and I know he would have put me through the wringer, but I would have shown him—" he rested his hands on her shoulders, now feeling the precious warmth of her through the silk of her dress "—I would have convinced him that I'm a man now, not a messed-up boy. I would have proven to him that I'm worthy of you, and if he didn't believe me, I'd have kept pounding away at it until he believed me. But he isn't here, so I talked to Marco, because he's sort of your father. He gave me his blessing, if that makes any difference, and threatened that if I ever hurt you he'd take me apart a piece at a time. Anyway, the point is…the point is that I love you, Sarah Gallagher."

His hands drifted up to the cloud of soft hair and he

toyed with the silky strands before his fingers found her arms again.

Slowly he began to turn her around. Would he see rejection? Embarrassment? Worst of all pity? His stomach clenched into a solid knot.

Let it be love, he prayed. *Let me see love there.*

Inch by inch, he turned her until she was facing him. Her smile, her eyes, her soft exhalation. How he loved each and every atom of her, how he'd been a fool ever to risk losing her.

"I love you, Sarah," he whispered.

She studied his face, his eyes. "I didn't think you would ever say those words again."

Did she or didn't she? He was about to explode, on tenterhooks of fear. "Sarah?"

"I love you, too, Dominic Jett." She took his face in her hands and pressed her lips to his. Joy ebbed like a roaring tide inside him until he thought he would burst.

"How could this be real?" she breathed.

He was barely able to answer. "I guess it's true what they say about God working in mysterious ways." He kissed her again, molding her into his arms.

"Nothing more mysterious than a kibble-carrying chocolate hater."

He threw back his head and laughed, long and loud, amazed that he felt lighter than air, as if he had overcome the chains that bound him and reached the pinnacle. He fumbled in his pocket for a ring, a slender gold band with no more than a diamond chip on it. "I'm going to get you a better one, when I have the money, but for now…will this do?"

She blinked hard as he slid the ring on her finger. "It will do just fine. Forever. I love you, Jett," she said, one crystal tear trailing down her perfect cheek.

He caught that tear with his fingertip and made a vow to himself that he would be there to catch every tear, every peal of laughter, the good, the difficult and everything in between. "Oh, Sarah Gal, how did I ever think I could live without you?"

He kissed her then, and he knew he'd finally made it home.

* * * * *

Dear Reader,

While I hope you have not been in the same situation as Jett and Sarah as they struggle to get free from two powerful enemies, I know we've all experienced what it's like to have our lives take an unexpected turn. It's so easy to question God's love for us when all we can see is monumental obstacles all around. Jett has a similar feeling, dealing with his troubled family history and failed career. It comforts me to know that while I may not triumph over the roadblocks in my way, God has already overcome. He wins, and when we choose to believe and follow, we win, too. What a wonderful encouragement to us, don't you think? I hope this story provides you with some excitement, refreshment and a renewed sense of how very precious you are to God.

Thank you for taking the time to read my book. As always, I welcome comments to my website, Facebook and Twitter accounts. If you prefer to correspond by mail, there is a physical address listed on my website. God bless!

Fondly,

Dana Mentink

COMING NEXT MONTH FROM
Love Inspired® Suspense

Available December 6, 2016

ROOKIE K-9 UNIT CHRISTMAS
Rookie K-9 Unit • by Lenora Worth and Valerie Hansen
When danger strikes at Christmastime, two K-9 police officers meet their perfect matches in these exciting, brand-new novellas.

CLASSIFIED CHRISTMAS MISSION
Wrangler's Corner • by Lynette Eason
On the run to protect her late best friend's child, who may have witnessed his mother's murder, former spy Amber Starke returns to her hometown. But with the killer on her heels, she'll have to trust local deputy Lance Goode to help them survive.

CHRISTMAS CONSPIRACY
First Responders • by Susan Sleeman
When Rachael Long unmasks a would-be kidnapper after he breaks into her day care and tries to abduct a baby, she becomes his new target. But with first response squad commander Jake Marsh guarding her, she just might evade the killer's grasp.

STALKING SEASON
Smoky Mountain Secrets • by Sandra Robbins
Cheyenne Cassidy believes the stalker who killed her parents is dead—until he follows her into the Smoky Mountains and shatters her hopes of beginning a new life. Now Cheyenne must rely on Deputy Sheriff Luke Conrad to keep her safe from an obsessed murderer.

HAZARDOUS HOLIDAY
Men of Valor • by Liz Johnson
In order to help his cousin's struggling widow and her seriously ill son, navy SEAL Zach McCloud marries Kristi Tanner. And when he returns home from a mission to find that someone wants them dead, he'll do anything to save his temporary family.

MISTLETOE REUNION THREAT
Rangers Under Fire • by Virginia Vaughan
After assistant district attorney Ashlynn Morris's son goes missing, she turns to former army ranger Garrett Lewis—her ex-fiancé and the father of her child—for help finding him. But can Garrett keep Ashlynn alive long enough to rescue the son he never knew he had?

REQUEST YOUR FREE BOOKS!
2 FREE RIVETING INSPIRATIONAL NOVELS
PLUS 2 FREE MYSTERY GIFTS

Love Inspired
SUSPENSE
RIVETING INSPIRATIONAL ROMANCE

YES! Please send me 2 FREE Love Inspired® Suspense novels and my 2 FREE mystery gifts (gifts are worth about $10). After receiving them, if I don't wish to receive any more books, I can return the shipping statement marked "cancel." If I don't cancel, I will receive 4 brand-new novels every month and be billed just $4.99 per book in the U.S. or $5.49 per book in Canada. That's a savings of at least 17% off the cover price. It's quite a bargain! Shipping and handling is just 50¢ per book in the U.S. and 75¢ per book in Canada.* I understand that accepting the 2 free books and gifts places me under no obligation to buy anything. I can always return a shipment and cancel at any time. Even if I never buy another book, the two free books and gifts are mine to keep forever.

123/323 IDN GH5Z

Name _____ (PLEASE PRINT) _____

Address _____ Apt. # _____

City _____ State/Prov. _____ Zip/Postal Code _____

Signature (if under 18, a parent or guardian must sign) _____

Mail to the **Reader Service:**
IN U.S.A.: P.O. Box 1867, Buffalo, NY 14240-1867
IN CANADA: P.O. Box 609, Fort Erie, Ontario L2A 5X3

Are you a current subscriber to Love Inspired® Suspense books
and want to receive the larger-print edition?
Call 1-800-873-8635 or visit www.ReaderService.com.

* Terms and prices subject to change without notice. Prices do not include applicable taxes. Sales tax applicable in N.Y. Canadian residents will be charged applicable taxes. Offer not valid in Quebec. This offer is limited to one order per household. Not valid for current subscribers to Love Inspired Suspense books. All orders subject to credit approval. Credit or debit balances in a customer's account(s) may be offset by any other outstanding balance owed by or to the customer. Please allow 4 to 6 weeks for delivery. Offer available while quantities last.

Your Privacy—The Reader Service is committed to protecting your privacy. Our Privacy Policy is available online at www.ReaderService.com or upon request from the Reader Service.
We make a portion of our mailing list available to reputable third parties that offer products we believe may interest you. If you prefer that we not exchange your name with third parties, or if you wish to clarify or modify your communication preferences, please visit us at www.ReaderService.com/consumerschoice or write to us at Reader Service Preference Service, P.O. Box 9062, Buffalo, NY 14240-9062. Include your complete name and address.

LIS15

SPECIAL EXCERPT FROM

Love Inspired
SUSPENSE

*When a CIA agent goes on the run home,
she'll need help from the local deputy to keep a
vulnerable young charge alive.*

Read on for a preview of
CLASSIFIED CHRISTMAS MISSION
by **Lynette Eason**, *the next exciting book in the*
WRANGLER'S CORNER *series!*

Deputy Lance Goode caught sight of headlights just ahead on the sharp curve and slowed. He focused on staying on his side of the road. The headlights came closer. Followed by a second set. Who was crazy enough to be out in this mess besides him?

He passed the first car and blinked. Even through the falling snow, he'd caught a glimpse of the driver. Amber Starke?

A loud crack split the quiet mountainside, and Lance stepped on the brakes. Chills swept over him. He'd heard that sound before. A gunshot.

When he looked back he saw Amber's SUV spin and then plunge over the side of the mountain. The vehicle behind her never stopped, just roared past.

Lance pulled to a stop. He headed to the edge to look over. He saw the tracks disappear under an overhang. Relief shot through him. Amber's sedan had only gone down the slight slope, under the overhang, and wedged itself between two trees. Now he just had to find out if the bullet had done any bodily damage.

He ran to his SUV and opened the back. He grabbed the hundred-foot-length rope that he always carried with him and hefted it over his shoulder. He lugged it to the front of the Ford and tied one end to the grill then tossed the rest down to Amber's car. It reached, but barely. With one more glance over his shoulder, he grasped hold of the rope and slipped and slid down the embankment to the car. He was able to duck under the overhang and squeeze himself between the rock and the driver's door.

Amber lay against the wheel, eyes closed. Fear shot through. *Please let her be all right.* He reached for the door handle and pulled it open. It hit the rock, but there was enough room for her to get out if she wasn't too badly hurt.

Amber lifted her head and he found himself staring down the barrel of a gun.

Don't miss
CLASSIFIED CHRISTMAS MISSION
by Lynette Eason, available wherever
Love Inspired® Suspense books and ebooks are sold.

www.LoveInspired.com

Love Inspired

Love the Love Inspired book you just read?

Your opinion matters.

Review this book on your favorite book site, review site, blog or your own social media properties and share your opinion with other readers!